HOPE RESTORED

A GALLAGHER BROTHERS NOVEL

CARRIE ANN RYAN

Hope Restored
A Gallagher Brothers Novel
By: Carrie Ann Ryan
© 2017 Carrie Ann Ryan
ISBN: 978-1-943123-58-2
Cover Art by Charity Hendry
Photograph ©2016 Jenn LeBlanc / Illustrated Romance

For more information, please join Carrie Ann Ryan's
MAILING LIST
To interact with Carrie Ann Ryan, you can join her
FAN CLUB.

PRAISE FOR CARRIE ANN RYAN....

"Carrie Ann Ryan knows how to pull your heartstrings and make your pulse pound! Her wonderful Redwood Pack series will draw you in and keep you reading long into the night. I can't wait to see what comes next with the new generation, the Talons. Keep them coming, Carrie Ann!" – Lara Adrian, New York Times bestselling author of CRAVE THE NIGHT

"Carrie Ann Ryan never fails to draw readers in with passion, raw sensuality, and characters that pop off the page. Any book by Carrie Ann is an absolute treat." – New York Times Bestselling Author J. Kenner

"With snarky humor, sizzling love scenes, and brilliant, imaginative worldbuilding, The Dante's Circle series reads as if Carrie Ann Ryan peeked at my personal wish list!" – NYT Bestselling Author, Larissa Ione

"Carrie Ann Ryan writes sexy shifters in a world full of

passionate happily-ever-afters." – *New York Times* Bestselling Author Vivian Arend

"Once again, Carrie Ann Ryan knocks the Dante's Circle series out of the park. The queen of hot, sexy, enthralling paranormal romance, Carrie Ann is an author not to miss!" *New York Times* bestselling Author Marie Harte

DEDICATION

To Dr. Hubby.
This year, man. This year.
We'll get through it.
Together.

ACKNOWLEDGMENTS

Writing this book was a lesson in heartache and determination. My worlds collided and Murphy and Tessa's book ended up being a way to heal not only my own wounds, but those of a few others close in my life.

I know I couldn't have written this book without so many, so bear with me while I do my list thing that I adore and thank those who helped me set aside so many parts of my life so I could give Murphy and Tessa their due.

Thank you Chelle for not only sitting with me when we broke ourselves over this plot, but by putting your all in our edits. Thank you Charity for a kickass cover and Tara for getting the word out when all I wanted to do was write some more. Thank you Cathy and Karin for being my final betas. Thank you Dr. Hubby for being my rock and for letting me be yours.

Thank you dear readers for following me on this journey. I have fallen in love with the Gallagher Brothers and I'm so happy y'all have as well.

Happy reading!

~Carrie Ann

HOPE RESTORED

The Gallagher Brothers series from NYT Bestselling Author Carrie Ann Ryan concludes with the final brother who thought he had everything to look forward to, and the one woman who can handle him.

Life isn't worth living if you don't fight to live. That's what Murphy Gallagher learned at a young age when cancer ravaged his body not once, but twice. Over the course of his survival, he lost his parents and his childhood, but he's been healthy for years and has become a man he hopes his family is proud of. But when his world tilts on its axis yet again, he'll have to learn what it means to fight not only the unknown but also his attraction to his best friend.

Tessa Stone works hard and plays harder. She's spent her life trying to figure out who she is in the present rather than looking back. Yet when she's forced into close proximity with Murphy, she'll have to not only be his rock but learn how to relax enough to maybe let him be hers, as well. But seduction doesn't stop when the world seems to, and close encounters of the naked kind might just be the first step in something much more complicated than either of them bargained for. Life, though, is for living, after all.

1

Sometimes, life was damn good. Other times, it kicked him in the balls until he couldn't catch his breath. Today, luckily, was one of the good days. Murphy Gallagher grinned from ear to ear as he tried to run from his niece, Rowan. She was eleven now and getting pretty fast, but he was faster. Not that he'd actually run at his full speed around her. It was always more entertaining when she caught him and took him to her lair.

As he was the evil dragon to her warrior princess, it only made sense.

"Behold! My mighty sword that shall slay the dragon!"

Murphy bit his tongue so he wouldn't start laughing, but seriously, where had Rowan learned to say things like that? Of course, she was almost a teenager now and probably a little too old to play princess and the dragon, but that wasn't something Murphy would ever bring up. Her mom, Blake, had been married to Murphy's brother, Graham, for a little while now. Murphy hadn't known Rowan when she was little, and he had a lot of playing to catch up on being her favorite uncle.

Sure, his brothers Owen and Jake were decent uncles, as well, but he would always be the best. Jake was the artistic one, Owen the type-A, Graham the grumpy one, and Murphy was the fun one.

He had to play his part and make sure Rowan had the time of her life. She'd only had her mom to play with for years, and while Blake was a kickass mother who made sure Rowan had the best childhood, Murphy wanted to make sure Rowan had even more fun now.

Murphy rolled to the ground as Rowan jumped on his back, both of them laughing so hard they shook. He made sure to take the brunt of the impact so he wouldn't hurt his niece. She giggled as she stabbed him with her imaginary sword, and he put his hand over his heart and gasped, feigning injury before letting his tongue hang out and groaning.

And...the dragon was dead.

"Victory!" Rowan stood up and started dancing near Murphy's corpse like any dignified warrior princess was wont to do.

"It's about time," Graham said with a laugh as he walked out from the porch where the rest of the Gallaghers were sitting. "I thought you'd have gotten him within the first few minutes, Rowan."

Murphy sat up as Rowan beamed at her stepdad, though she just called him "Dad" now. Murphy smiled as he remembered the first time Rowan had called his brother "Dad" in front of them. Every single Gallagher had choked up and didn't bother shrugging it off. They might all be inked, bearded, and pierced, but Rowan referring to Graham as her father as if it were no big deal was a big fucking deal.

"I didn't want my prey to feel like it didn't put up a fight," Rowan said solemnly.

Murphy barked a laugh. "Prey? Really? What shows are you watching these days?"

Rowan turned to him and rolled her eyes with the pro of a teenage girl, rather than the eleven-year-old she was. "It was from a book, *duh*. Uncle Border got me a whole set of books with dragons in them."

Border was Jake's husband and the quietest of their group, though Murphy knew Border and Jake's wife, Maya, was slowly changing that. The triad had been together the longest out of the Gallagher relationships, and yet they still acted like newlyweds with the way they incessantly groped one another.

Come to think of it, Blake and Graham acted the same way. And, hell, Owen and Liz—newly engaged—made out relentlessly, as well. No wonder Liz and Blake were pregnant; their men couldn't keep their hands off their women.

That, of course, meant that Murphy was the last single Gallagher. He didn't mind, though. After all, someone had to bear the mantle of bachelorhood. Plus, he really wasn't ready to start settling down yet. He'd just learned to live life as it was, no need to change everything so dramatically again.

And that was enough of that.

Murphy rolled his shoulders and took Graham's outstretched hand, helping him to his feet. "It wasn't *Game of Thrones* was it?" he asked his niece.

Rowan rolled her eyes again, and Graham narrowed his. "It wasn't *that,* Uncle Murphy."

"What did we say about rolling your eyes so much, Rowan? Use your words, not your attitude."

Rowan blushed and looked down at her feet. "Sorry, Dad."

Murphy did his best not to smile at the way Graham's chest puffed out at that. Seriously, the man was like a damn peacock. And now that Blake was pregnant, his brother was even worse. It was as if he were the first man to get his wife pregnant. And considering Jake and Border already had a kid with Maya, and Owen's fiancée Liz was also pregnant, it wasn't as if babies were something totally new to their crew.

Though with the way everyone kept popping them out, Murphy made a mental note to buy more condoms. There was something in the water with all the pregnancy hormones flying around like they were.

Murphy followed father and daughter back to the porch and gingerly took a seat next to Liz's former roommate and Owen's neighbor, Tessa—the only other single person at the

Gallagher family dinner. He'd hit the ground a bit hard when he rolled to make sure Rowan didn't get hurt in her exuberance and now his muscles were feeling it. He was in damned good shape—had to be for his job—but, apparently, he needed more protein or something because his body made him feel like an old man.

Murphy looked at the brunette next to him. Tessa wasn't a Gallagher, but she was the only family Liz had, even though they weren't related by blood. Plus, it would have been awkward as hell to *not* have Tessa over since there wasn't a fence separating the two yards at the moment. Owen had taken it down after a few of the boards rotted. Eventually, they'd put it back up.

Considering that the family owned a construction and restoration company, it wouldn't take too long, but they actually had to find the time to do it. Murphy figured he'd be enlisted soon to take care of it since he was the only one without a pregnant significant other or kids to keep him busy. And it wasn't like he minded. He liked being able to do things for his family since they'd spent so much of their lives doing things for him when he couldn't do them for himself.

And that, once again, was enough of those thoughts.

"You okay, dear dragon?" Tessa asked with a wink before handing over a beer.

He took it with a wink of his own. "Thanks, and yeah. That warrior princess is tough."

She laughed and pulled her long, chestnut hair behind

her shoulders. He hadn't seen her wear it down for a while since she was always working and tended to do severe ponytails. He had to say, he kind of liked it better down. Not that he'd tell her that since she'd have his balls for breakfast if he did. Every single woman in the Gallagher's circle tended to be a ballbuster, and while Murphy loved it, he didn't want to lose his nuts. He liked them, what could he say.

"That she is, but I was serious. You hit the ground hard, and you winced when you sat down. Did you hurt yourself? Because you know, Murphy Gallagher, you may still be hot as fuck, but you're not getting any younger." She whispered the last part so the kids wouldn't hear, and Murphy held back a snort.

Considering he'd spent most of his life praying that he'd have a chance to *get* older, he didn't mind that he had a few more aches and pains now that he was in his thirties. Hell, he'd relish the day he got wrinkles and grey in his hair. That meant he was *alive* to witness his body changing. For a man who didn't know if that would ever happen, it was his own form of bliss.

Of course, he didn't tell Tessa any of that and wasn't sure why he'd let his thoughts get that deep so suddenly. Tessa was a fantastic person and sexy as all get out, and he *loved* flirting with her, but there was no way he'd get into deep feelings or heavy conversation with her. Their dynamic worked because they joked around and kept things light—if a bit inappropriate at times. If he changed that, then things would get fucked up, and he didn't want to jeopardize what they had. Hell, he didn't want to jeopardize her position in the group.

Everything was better if they just remained friends that didn't go too deep.

"Hey, Murphy, did you send over the files on the house?" Owen asked, a frown on his face as he looked at his phone. Liz was perched on his lap, their hands tangled over her baby bump. She was finally starting to show, and Murphy loved the way she glowed. She just finally seemed so at peace with being pregnant, though he knew that wasn't always the case since the baby hadn't exactly been planned.

He made another note to himself to buy condoms. He couldn't be too careful these days.

"I did," he answered before pulling out his phone to check his outgoing messages. "I thought you replied back."

Owen let out a sigh. "Shit, I did. Sorry. Didn't get much sleep last night."

Murphy looked over at Tessa and winked since she loved joking with him, and she laughed before whistling. "What were you doing, Mr. Organized One, if you weren't sleeping."

Owen looked over to where Rowan held her cousin Noah, Jake's son, and shook his head. "Perv," his brother whispered. "I was up finishing the final details on Blake's house."

Blake looked over and widened her eyes. "It's almost done? Really?"

Murphy didn't blame his sister-in-law for the incredu-

lous look. The Gallaghers had been working on Blake's
family home for over a year now and had hit every obstacle
known to man, including a kidnapping and an injured
worker thanks to Blake's former in-laws. Murphy fisted his
hands as he let the rage wash through him, remembering
everything that Graham and Blake had gone through when
they were dating.

"It's almost done," Graham said as he wrapped his arm
around Blake's middle, his large hand resting over Blake's
tiny baby bump. She wasn't as far along as Liz, but she
was close.

Blake wiped away tears and turned into Graham's arms
for a hug. Murphy blinked in surprise at Blake's show of
emotion since she usually hid what she felt so well. Either
she was feeling more comfortable around them, or it was
the baby hormones. Knowing Blake, it might be a little
of both.

"I can't believe it's almost done," Blake said after a
moment. "I mean, I knew you had to be close, but..." She
shook her head as if at a loss for words.

Maya came up and hugged Blake, even though Graham
refused to let his wife go. "These guys are pretty amazing,
aren't they? And soon, you won't have to deal with the house
at all. It'll be in the city's hands and only a distant memory."
She kissed Blake's temple before going back to take Noah
out of Rowan's arms.

Murphy didn't know the whole story behind Blake's
childhood, but he knew it wasn't good. She'd grown up

affluent but with the worst kind of family. She'd run off as soon as she could, and had had Rowan when she was pretty young. And when her parents had died, they'd left the huge mansion in disrepair and neglect but had forced Blake through their will to oversee the restoration. The project had brought Graham and Blake together, but other than that, it had been a pain in the ass. And considering that Murphy loved jobs where he got to dive into the history of a place and see how to keep some of the past blended into the present, it was saying something that he truly wanted nothing more to do with the project.

The others began talking about the next steps involved in finishing up the house as well as what they would do next since their last big project hadn't panned out thanks to shady deals and selfish businessmen. But Murphy just closed his eyes and let the breeze slide over him. He'd slept for shit the night before, and he wished it had been because of a woman. Instead, he hadn't been feeling well and had tossed and turned all night.

"Hey, I'm going to go get the chips and salsa, want to help?" Tessa asked. She put her hand on his forearm, and he opened his eyes. Her hands were cold to the touch, but it could be that his skin was overheated. Ever since the chemo when he was younger, he had a hard time keeping a consistent body temperature. That's what happened when you had leukemia when you were in grade school and again when you were a teenager. You dealt with the side effects for the rest of your life.

No wonder he was damn tired.

"Sure," he said and sat up, taking a sip of his beer once he was on his feet. The others were still shooting the breeze and passing Noah around. The kid was getting pretty big since he was nearing one year old now. Or at least Murphy thought. He should probably check his calendar and make sure he hadn't missed a birthday since their family kept growing.

He and Tessa made their way to the kitchen and got out the chips and three kinds of salsa and dip that they'd made for the barbeque. Tessa brushed by him on her way to the fridge, and his cock hardened.

He glared down at his crotch, annoyed with himself for once again getting hard around her. She was his *friend*. Sure, they flirted because it was fun, but they'd never fooled around, and there was no way they would now. They'd firmly put themselves into their roles, and he didn't want to change that.

Of course, his dick had other ideas, but hell, Tessa was *hot*. She was tall, mostly leg, and had just enough curves that he knew he'd have plenty to hold onto when he fucked her from behind or held her up against the wall and pounded into her.

Not when.

Never.

He would *never* be fucking Tessa against anything, thank you very much.

Tessa snuck a chip into the salsa and groaned. He did

his best not to think about whether she'd groan like that under him, or over him...anywhere around him.

"This is so good. Here, taste." She held out a chip with salsa on it, and he bent forward, taking it in one bite as he gently nipped at her fingers.

She swallowed hard before lowering her hand and giving him a sultry smile. "Like it?"

He nodded before swallowing. "Spicy."

"I like a little heat, what can I say."

He snorted and took a sip of his beer. He loved flirting with Tessa, even though he had to use his hands more often than not when she wasn't around because she kept him in a perpetual state of arousal. He couldn't help it. She was sexy and flirted better than anyone he'd ever met, but still, they were just friends.

Tessa took his beer from him since she hadn't brought hers with her and took a sip, her eyes on him the whole time. He cleared his throat and looked away, only to glance at her breasts and notice that her nipples were hard pebbles against her *very* thin bra.

Damn, he could just bend her over the kitchen island and fuck her right there. Just slide her jeans down and fill that tight pussy with his dick. She'd cream for him, coming hard on his cock, and he'd fill her to the brim.

And...that wouldn't be happening.

He shook off those thoughts, and Tessa gave him a knowing wink before handing back his beer. He took a deep swallow, finishing it off, and then tossed the bottle into the recycling can.

"Why didn't you bring Brian?" he asked, keeping his mind on what was important. Like the fact that she was sort of dating a guy that wasn't him.

Tessa laughed and picked up one of the trays of veggies they'd also taken out of the fridge. "His name is Brent, dork. We're not that serious and still pretty new. There's no way I'd bring him over to one of these. We're just casual. And why didn't you bring one of your many lady friends?"

"There aren't that many, and I'm not seeing anyone serious right now." In fact, now that he thought about it, he hadn't been with a woman in over a month. Hell, no wonder he couldn't get sex with Tessa off his mind. He just needed to get laid, and everything would work itself out.

Thoughts of Tessa just might kill him, but damn, he loved being her friend. Way better than any fucking amazing sex they might have.

"You're never seeing anyone serious, Murph. It's why we get along. Let the others be adults and get settled. We can live it up for the rest of them."

She turned and sashayed from the room, and he did his best to keep his eyes off her very bitable ass. It wasn't exactly easy since it was *right* there and practically speaking in tongues at him.

He followed Tessa out to the back deck and bent over the table to set everything down. He froze at Tessa's gasp and looked over his shoulder.

"What is it?"

"What the fuck, Murphy?" she asked, pulling up his shirt. "What happened to you?"

He frowned and straightened, trying to see what the hell she was talking about. "Huh?"

"Jesus Christ," Jake said shakily. "Your back, Murph. You're black and blue."

"What's wrong with Uncle Murphy?" Rowan asked, her voice shaky.

Thunder pounded in Murphy's ears, and he tried to process what everyone was saying, but they were all talking at once and trying to tug up his shirt. He pulled away from them and ran back into the house and into the nearest guest bathroom so he could check himself out in the mirror.

They had to be wrong or just fucking with him. Everything was fine. He was *not* black and blue. There was no way this could be happening again. He was healthy, damn it, and had been for a decade.

He wasn't sick.

He wasn't bruised.

But when he turned on the light and lifted up his shirt, he couldn't think. Couldn't speak. He'd looked at himself that morning after he got out of the shower, and the bruises hadn't been here. Yet his side and what he could see of his back were covered in newly formed bruises. They weren't bad yet, but he knew they'd grow.

They always did.

"Murphy," Tessa whispered from the doorway. "I... Murphy..."

He met her eyes in the mirror and tried to think of something to say to brush this off, but he couldn't. He knew what the bruises meant. He'd seen them before. Every single little ache and pain, infected scratch from the jobsite, mood swing, and fever over the past few weeks came back to him in a rush.

His cancer was back.

And he had no idea what the fuck he was going to do about it.

2

Tessa Stone loved and hated her job. It depended on the day and the department she worked with, but mostly, she loved it. Today, however, she couldn't keep her mind on her work. Instead, she kept thinking about the fact that Murphy was sick, and there was nothing she could do about it.

She worked in the administrative and financial department of a major hospital, so being around sick people wasn't new to her. However, actually knowing the person and truly caring about said person wasn't even in the same ballpark for her.

She hadn't meant to blurt out what she'd seen like she did, but she'd been so shocked at his bruises that she'd forgotten where she was. So instead of calmly taking him aside and asking him if his back hurt, she'd pointed out that he was a mess of bruises to his whole family.

16 CARRIE ANN RYAN

And the entire Gallagher clan had freaked out with her, and it had probably made things worse for Murphy. It was apparent he hadn't known he'd bruised so easily after wrestling on the ground with Rowan. Tessa's honorary niece had been distraught, blaming herself for hurting her dragon and favorite uncle and had had to be taken home when she wouldn't stop sobbing and hiding from Murphy. As if he'd blame her. The party had broken up quickly after the others met her and Murphy in the bathroom, concern in their eyes and tones.

Murphy had promised to call his oncologist and hematologist right away to set up an appointment. That had been five days ago. She hadn't heard a thing from him or anyone else for that matter. She knew she wasn't related to them, but she had hoped that *someone* would have filled her in on how the appointment went and if they had any news. For all she knew, Murphy had just bruised randomly, and everything was fine. But she had a feeling from everyone's reaction—including his—that it wouldn't be that easy. She knew he'd had leukemia as a kid at least once, and though his kind had been treatable, those things tended to come back. And the chances of getting another type were also higher.

She just hoped that she was wrong and everything was fine.

It had to be.

"Ms. Stone, I need the Lane file. Do you have it handy?" Tessa looked up as her co-worker, Roger Sanders, tapped his finger on the desk in front of her. She didn't know why the man refused to call her by her first name, but she went with it. Maybe he didn't like women in places of authority since she was at the same level as he was, and that meant they were higher up in the admin levels. Or maybe he was just really formal. Either way, she called him Mr. Sanders, sounding a bit snooty since calling each other by their surnames was a little weird.

She might wear suits and keep her hair and makeup purely professional, but beneath the cashmere and neutral tones, she was still Tessa Stone, snark queen, and temptress.

She slid the file over and tapped a few things on her tablet, pushing thoughts of Murphy out of her mind. She'd always worry about him because he was her friend, but she had to focus on her work for now. Once she was finished for the day, she'd find out what she could about him.

"Thank you, Ms. Stone." Roger turned without another glance, and she raised her brows.

"You're welcome, Mr. Sanders," she mumbled and went through the rest of her files for the day. Her job was to make sure that people's insurance covered everything possible. Yes, some in her position might see themselves as the ones making sure the hospital got paid, but Tessa did her best to think of it as the opposite. She wanted the insurance companies to pay, not the patients, and if she had to work overtime hours finding every damn loophole she could, she would. Healthcare in this country was ridiculous, and she refused to be part of the problem.

That brought her back to the fact that she both loved and hated her job. It used to be more love when Liz worked as a nurse down in the ER. But when the hospital had downsized, and Liz lost her job due to politics and the damn bitches that worked downstairs, Tessa had lost one of the main reasons she enjoyed working there.

Her best friend was now a nurse at a local, private oncology office that was run by a brother of one of the ER doctors. Liz was just starting out there, but Tessa could see that her best friend was made for that job. It wasn't as stressful, and she could work normal hours. That was a great thing since Liz and Owen were planning a wedding and going to be parents soon. Her friend had been taking a few classes and certification placements since she'd lost her job so she'd be completely ready for her new one, and Tessa had never been prouder.

Of course, thinking about the oncology clinic just made her think of Murphy, and she sighed. It seemed that until she knew exactly what was wrong with her friend, she wouldn't be able to think straight.

So she rolled her shoulders and gave her best to her patients while trying not to think the worst. And when the clock hit six, she packed up her things and headed to her car, cursing herself when she remembered that she needed to change before she left.

She'd forgotten that she promised Brent she would meet him at the winery he'd been talking about for a while now. She looked down at her beige skirt and white top and shrugged. She could fit in with a winery crowd, so she might as well save time and go as she was. She wouldn't even bother to let her hair down since that would just take time, and frankly, she wasn't in the mood for tonight anyway. But Brent had been looking forward to this, and though they weren't serious, she didn't want to disappoint him.

She just wished he'd wanted to go to a brewery or something. That was much more her style, but dating required compromise. She wasn't sure why she was with Brent, but she'd promised herself she would try being with a nice guy for once. Dating random so-called bad boys hadn't made her life any better and had only gone to show her that she needed to look beyond her comfort zone.

Brent was a nice guy, though he was *boring*. Liz joked that Tessa had enough energy for both of them, so maybe that would be enough. He was okay in bed if a little...uncreative, but then again, Tessa tended to find faults with every guy she dated. So she would stick with Brent for a bit longer until she was sure she wasn't being hasty by cutting him loose.

She pulled up to the winery and turned off her car, checking her phone for any missed messages. She had one from Brent, letting her know he'd just arrived and would be waiting inside, but that was it. Liz and the Gallaghers hadn't called her, and she was starting to feel a little left out. No, this wasn't about her, but she wanted to know what was going on, and she'd done her best not to crowd Murphy. She'd seen the way he became overwhelmed with so many people looking after him, and she'd tried to give him space. It just sucked that she didn't know what was going on. Though even if she did, what could she do? How would she help him?

Her phone buzzed again, and she looked down only to see it was Brent saying that he'd seen her pull in and couldn't wait to see her.

See? Such a nice guy.

And, well...she wasn't the nice girl.

Memories of what had happened the last time she'd tried to be the nice girl filled her mind, and she quickly pushed those thoughts away. She stuffed her phone in her bag, reapplied her matte lipstick, and rolled her shoulders. Time to taste some wine and spit it into a bucket like some heathen or something and then go home.

Her brain wasn't in gear tonight, and she had a feeling she wouldn't want to sleep with Brent tonight...not with her mind on another man.

She wasn't that horrible of a person.

At least, she hoped.

TESSA PULLED into her driveway a couple of hours later, starving and pissed at herself for not sneaking more of those tiny appetizers the winery had served. They'd been air-filled pockets with no flavor, but eventually, with enough of them, they might have filled her stomach. She hadn't thought to pick up a burger or something on the way to the winery, and apparently, everyone else had been fine sipping wine and eating next to nothing. Brent only sipped a few varieties before switching to water since he was driving and responsible. As Tessa also refused to drive even slightly tipsy, she'd eaten what she could and hadn't bothered with more than a sip or two of wine. She didn't like the stuff anyway, but Brent had wanted to try it out.

Now, she was starving, a little on edge, and kind of disappointed that Brent hadn't even offered to follow her home and have his way with her. Instead, he'd kissed her softly on the lips in the parking lot—without copping a feel, mind you—and had asked her to text him when she got home to ensure that she was safe. He was just so *nice.* It did nothing for her libido.

But there was more to life than orgasms. At least, that's what she'd heard on TV.

So, she texted him quickly from the car that she was home and safe, and he sent a smiling emoji back. With a sigh, she sent a wink one his way and got out of the car. He didn't respond to that with some quip like Murphy would have, and she shoved away the disappointment again.

Casual, she reminded herself. She and Brent were casual and had both said they might be dating other people. So why did she feel bad for flirting with Murphy? Maybe because she knew nothing would ever come of it. It was *safe* flirting with him because he gave it just as hard back, and she knew she wouldn't end up breaking it off with him in the end like she did with so many others.

Man, she really needed food in her stomach because her brain was going in too many weird directions tonight. She made her way up her small porch and turned the key in her lock, freezing when the hairs on the back of her neck stood on end. It felt as if someone were watching her, but that didn't make any sense. They were in a safe neighborhood, and all the lights were off at Liz and Owen's next door so it couldn't be them.

She checked behind her before quickly going inside and locking the door. Her chest rose and fell in pants, and she did up the chain before going to make sure the house was empty. She was just freaking herself out for no reason, but still, she needed to be safe. She pulled the Taser out of her purse just to err on the side of caution. She was a woman living alone now and had been through enough to know that she needed to take care of herself. Her house, of course, was empty, and she frowned when she passed Liz's now vacant room.

She missed her best friend and hated that they were going through the process of changing the mortgage so it was in Tessa's name alone. It had been her idea since Liz wouldn't be living there anymore, but she'd kind of thought they would own the house together a bit longer. As it was, she knew that her budget would be tight for a bit—maybe longer than a bit if she were honest, since the housing market in Denver was crazy at the moment. It didn't matter, though, and she put the thought aside as she pulled out leftover takeout from the fridge and started to heat it up. Liz was living her dream—a dream she hadn't even realized she had—and Tessa was growing up and dating a good man.

Finally, she figured her parents would say.

THE MICROWAVE BEEPED, and she took out the container and started munching on fried rice. She toed off her heels and looked down at her phone before saying *screw it* and hitting Murphy's name on her recent calls list.

She had to know what was going on, and if that made her selfish, well, she'd figure out a way to atone for it.

"Hey, Legs, what's up?"

She smiled at the sound of his voice before shaking that off. Weird. "Legs? Is that what you're calling me now?"

"Your legs go on for miles, so yeah, Legs works."

"I'd ask what to call you, but you'd probably end up with like Big D or something."

Murphy barked out a laugh, and she grinned as she stuffed her mouth with fried rice. She was seriously starving. "So, what's up?"

"That's what I wanted to ask you." Silence. "Damn it. I shouldn't have called and gotten all up in your business, but you worried me this weekend. If I'm pushing, just tell me. I tend to push, and need boundaries set. Something you know about me." He didn't speak, so she barreled on, making a fool of herself. "Did you see your doctor?"

"I did."

She swallowed hard, the rice now a ball of regret in her belly. "Yeah?"

"Shit, I figured Liz would have told you by now."

She shook her head, tears filling her eyes, then remembered he couldn't see her. "No one's told me anything. Maybe they didn't want to share your business."

"You can know anything you want about me, Tessa. You know that."

Did she?

"Murph..."

"It's back."

Her knees went weak, and she sank to the kitchen floor, her food forgotten. "What's back?"

"They're still running tests, and I actually get to meet with Liz's boss this upcoming week to discuss options since my insurance company will thankfully let me use the clinic, but we're pretty sure it's CLL."

"Chronic Lymphocytic Leukemia." She said the words slowly, her heart beating fast in her chest.

"I forget you work in a hospital and would know that." His voice was a little hollow, and she wanted to reach through the phone and hold him, telling him everything would be okay. Since she couldn't do that, she tried to focus on what she knew.

"Do they have a prognosis?"

"Not yet. CLL is treatable and slow growing. It's not what I had as a kid since this is chronic and a little different. Apparently, one percent of people who had the kind of chemo I did can develop CLL later. Lucky me. I'm going to beat it, though. Damn it. I think Owen already has a few notebooks of research, so I'll be doing a lot of reading."

She swallowed hard, doing her best to keep her emotions in check. Murphy did not need another person overreacting or acting too emotional. He needed his flirty friend, and that was just who she'd be.

"Reading? Oh, dear. That sounds tough. Maybe you should get someone to read it to you. Maybe Rowan?"

"You can't see me, but I'm flipping you off right now."

"Good to know you still have your sense of humor. Just trying to cheer you up, you know? I'd try phone sex, but I don't want to overstimulate you."

She froze, her eyes going wide. *What the fuck, Tessa?*

Murphy laughed hard into the phone, and she relaxed. "You know, you're the first person to make me laugh since this weekend. So, thank you." He yawned, and she pressed her lips together, trying not to think about why he'd be so tired already. "I should get some sleep."

She closed her eyes, finding her strength. "I guess I should, too. Just... Murphy? If you need me, I'm here. And not just for jokes about sex, okay?"

He was silent a bit longer, and she was afraid she'd overstepped again. "Thanks, Tessa. And, yeah, once I know more, I'll be sure to keep you in the loop. I've beaten shit like this—worse than this—before, you know? Not gonna let it get me down."

"Hell yeah."

Neither of them sounded too convinced.

They hung up soon after that, and she stared down at her phone, wondering what on earth she was going to do. She was only an admin in the financial department of the hospital. Every other person around Murphy had more experience and ways to help than she did.

But she'd do what she could because this was Murphy, and he deserved to live.

Not only that, but he deserved to *live*.

And if all she could do was make him laugh when the world seemed to fall apart around them, then that's what she'd do.

Always.

3

Murphy's day went from shittastic to royally fucked in the span of two phone calls. He hadn't slept well the night before since his mind kept going in way too many directions and formulating scenarios he'd rather not think about at all. He still couldn't quite believe he was sick again.

When he'd been younger, after the first time he went into remission, his parents had constantly hovered over him to ensure that they would know the exact time a warning sign popped up. Murphy had spent countless hours in doctor's offices for a mere sniffle while his older brothers never had to deal with that stress or overprotectiveness. His parents had soothed his brothers and had ensured that the other three Gallaghers were pampered when they were sick, of course, but the constant fear had always been about him.

The stress had eventually killed his parents.

Not that anyone actually said as much, but Murphy knew. There were only so many years a body could go on in a constant state of hyper-awareness and near panic that something would go wrong. Once Murphy had been healthy for a significant amount of time, his parents' bodies had simply given out. Heart attacks and brain aneurysms in two otherwise healthy people wasn't as common as movies made it out to be.

But because of that vigilance when Murphy was a kid, his parents had been the first to realize something was wrong with him as a teenager. The same cancer he'd had as a child had come back, only worse because he'd been a little older and his body a little more tired from fighting it off the first time.

He'd come out alive—if a little more weary—the second time, as well.

And maybe because of that, Murphy had ignored what had been staring him right in the face for so long now. He'd known he was a little more tired than usual and yet had just tried to sleep more, drink more caffeine, and push through it. When he'd started having more mood swings than normal, he'd attributed that to the fact that he was tired. After all, he worked a physically *and* mentally demanding job as the lead architect for Gallagher Brothers Restoration.

But now, he was sick. *Really* sick. He didn't know what the exact treatments would be, but he knew they wouldn't be a walk in the park. He had an appointment with his oncologist at the clinic in a couple of days, and there, they would decide what the best course of action would be. His former oncologist was retiring soon, so he'd needed a new one to work with anyway, and thankfully, Liz now worked in a clinic that could help him. She wouldn't be his nurse because of conflict of interest, but she'd be there if he needed her. Hell, his whole family would be there if he needed them.

Murphy frowned and looked at his reflection in the mirror. He didn't *feel* like he had cancer. He didn't feel any differently other than the fact that he had a ball of dread in his stomach. Maybe if he looked hard enough, he'd see it. See it and know that his body was once again trying to kill him and the only way to live was to put poison into his system and hope for the best.

The circles under his eyes were slightly darker than usual, but that could be from the lack of sleep the night before. He didn't have any bruises on his face and neck, and if he pulled up his shirt, he wouldn't see any on his front either. But when he'd gotten out of the shower that morning, he'd seen the bruises on his back, sides, and legs that mingled with his ink. There was no hiding from that, even if part of him wanted to.

He ran a hand through his hair, letting the long strands slide through his fingers. He had the shortest beard of his brothers but the longest hair. Would he lose it all again if he had chemo and radiation? *It doesn't matter*, he thought to himself. In the end, he'd deal with it, even if it sucked and would be a constant reminder that something was *wrong*.

Murphy let out a sigh and looked down at the phone he'd set on his dresser after his phone calls of the morning. The first had been from his doctor's office, ensuring that he knew what to bring for his upcoming appointment. The second made him want to throw his damn cell across the room. But since he was about to spend most—if not all—of his savings on medical bills since his insurance would only cover so much, he didn't want to waste money on a temper tantrum.

And now it seemed he would need to spend even *more* money on things outside of his control.

His damn landlord had called, telling him that they were moving back to Denver instead of staying on the west coast as planned. Unlike his brothers, Murphy rented a house instead of owning it. He'd been saving for a home of his own but hadn't found anything he liked enough to want to spend that much money on it. If he didn't like the bones of the house, he wasn't going to live there and have his name on the deed. He was an architect and could work with most anything, but something had to call to him if he planned to own it. Plus, he was younger than his brothers by enough years that he was just getting to a place where he *could* buy a home in this market.

Denver's housing market had hit a boom, and finding a place to rent these days was impossible. People were buying homes hours after they went on the market and paying way over the asking prices because there just weren't enough properties in neighborhoods people wanted to live in right now.

It was ridiculous, and Murphy had thought he'd gotten out of that for a while at least. His landlords up until now had lived in San Diego and had been decent on his rent. Murphy did most of the repairs on the house himself and billed them for parts since it was just easier for him to do it rather than haggle to find someone else. It wasn't a large place, but he didn't need much space. It was only him, after all, and he hadn't dated seriously enough for the size of the house to be a problem.

But now that his landlords were moving back and his lease was up at the end of the month, he only had two weeks to find a new place.

Fucking impossible.

He'd been living in the same house for over five years now, and it was always around this time that he signed a new, year-long contract. It drove him mad that things were always down to the wire, but he'd never had an inkling that things would change so dramatically this year.

He had no fucking idea what he was going to do. He had treatments starting soon, a new project on the docket at work, and now he had to find a place to live. His brothers might let him crash at their places, but he didn't want to do that. Jake, Maya, and Border had the room, but they also had Noah. Murphy wasn't sure staying with them would be a good idea since his immune system was bound to take a hit with any chemo or radiation he ended up needing, and being around children was just asking for germs. All of the kids, including the impending babies, would need to be around germs so they could build up their immune systems. It's how things worked in the world. But Murphy knew he couldn't be around that.

Plus, all of his loved ones would spend so much of their time worrying about him instead of dealing with their own lives that he was afraid they'd end up hurting themselves in the process. It had happened to his parents, and he'd be damned if it happened to his brothers and their significant others, as well.

He blew out a breath and stuffed his phone into his pocket then picked up his keys. He didn't know what to do, but standing here and worrying about it wasn't helping matters. So he'd go to the one person he knew who could help him make a damn list or something so he could figure out his options.

Owen.

He didn't need his brothers making decisions for him, but he could use the advice. Owen would help him clear his head because if Murphy stayed much longer in his bedroom staring at himself, he might just have a panic attack.

It was the weekend, and he knew all of his brothers should have been off work—except maybe Jake who was an artist and tended to keep his own hours since he worked from home. Yet when Murphy pulled into Owen's driveway, he frowned. There wasn't a vehicle outside the house, and Murphy remembered that only Liz's car could fit inside the garage since Owen's truck was a little too tall. It didn't look like anyone was home, and Murphy laid his head on the steering wheel, forcing his breathing to slow down.

He would *not* have a panic attack just because one of his big brothers wasn't there when he needed him. He hadn't called ahead, and that was on him. Murphy could have called or gone to any of his other brothers, but he wasn't sure what to do.

Instead, he turned to the right and saw Tessa's vehicle in her driveway and relaxed somewhat. He could talk to Tessa. She wouldn't hover or overreact. She might not be able to help him figure out what to do, but he needed to talk to someone, and he liked talking to her. Even though she perpetually made him hard as a rock, she also listened and made him laugh. He could definitely use that right now.

He turned off the engine and slid out of his truck before walking through the yard to Tessa's. He frowned when he noticed one of the plants on her porch browning and shook his head. Liz was the one with the greener thumb, and he remembered that Tessa had tried her best but wasn't really good at keeping plants alive. Now that Liz wasn't living there anymore, all the responsibility of owning the home fell on Tessa's shoulders. That really had to suck after only a short time of sharing the house. But that's what happened when one of the duo fell in love and moved out.

Murphy rang the doorbell and stuffed his hands into his pockets while he waited for Tessa to answer. It was only now that he thought about how weird this was. He'd never actually been to Tessa's place without anyone else there, let alone showing up unannounced, needing to talk about things he wasn't sure he could actually put into words.

He almost thought about ducking and running, but that would have been idiotic, so he waited until Tessa opened the door. Her brows lifted at the sight of him before she gave him a wide smile.

He really liked Tessa's smile. Those lips said so much, even without words. She could smile flirty, cat-like, sweet, happy, bright, and sarcastic, all with subtle variations. Not that he studied her lips often. Or at all. She was just his friend.

"Hey, you, what's going on?"

He shifted from foot to foot and decided to be honest rather than finding a better way to say that he was an idiot. "I needed to talk to Owen. Or someone, that is, and he and Liz don't appear to be home." He closed his eyes and held back a groan. "Though I didn't exactly call them or knock on their door to check. I just assumed and, apparently, I'm an idiot today."

Tessa gave him a small laugh as he opened his eyes, and she took a step back to let him inside. "Owen's truck isn't in the driveway, so I would assume they're both gone too since it's the weekend. And I think Liz mentioned something about going to the Farmer's Market in Westminster today since they have better produce. You want something to drink while you wait for them?"

He blew out a breath, wondering how she could be so

easygoing about letting him hang out here while waiting for someone else. There really was no one like Tessa. "Actually, I was kind of hoping I could talk to you."

Her eyes widened fractionally, and her smile changed to one he didn't recognize. It wasn't wrong, it just looked... surprised maybe?

"Oh, sure. I mean, totally."

There was the sound of a toilet flushing behind her, and Murphy met Tessa's gaze only to have her close her eyes and blow out a breath.

"Hey, babe, I can't find the replacement soap since I used the last of it to wash my hands. I didn't want to leave you without it next time you go in there." A tall man with sandy-blond hair and wide shoulders walked out of Tessa's bedroom, and Murphy figured this guy had to be Brandon. Or Brody. Or...Brent. Yeah, Brent.

It was a Saturday afternoon, and the man wore khakis. Pressed khakis.

Well, then.

"Shit, I didn't realize you had company." He kept his voice low, feeling like an idiot.

"It's only Brent." Tessa winced. "And I meant that better than it sounded," she said under her breath in a rush. "Brent, no worries on the soap. It's in the hall closet. And, hey, this is my friend Murphy. He's Owen's brother."

At Brent's frown, she continued, and Murphy stayed silent, not sure what to say. "Owen? Liz's fiancé?"

"Oh, yeah, sorry, I forgot." Brent smiled, and Murphy gave the man a nod.

"Murphy," Tessa continued, "this is my...this is Brent." She winced again, and this time, Murphy held back a laugh. He wasn't sure what she'd planned to call Brent, but since she didn't say "boyfriend," he figured they were still in the casual stages of their relationship.

But still, khakis-wearing Brent seemed like an okay guy, if a bit boring. Murphy held back a smile as he held out his hand for Brent. The other man shook it and nodded slowly.

"So, what brings you here?" Brent asked, wrapping his arm around Tessa's waist. She artfully dodged his hold and gestured toward the couch.

"Yeah, why don't you take a seat and talk if you want. Or we can just chat about random things while you wait for Owen and Liz to get home." She was giving him an out so he wouldn't have to speak about certain things in front of Brent, and for that, he was grateful. Yet he still felt like he was invading her space.

"I can come by another time," he said quickly. "I didn't mean to interrupt."

"You didn't." Tessa moved forward and pulled gently by him elbow as if she were afraid she'd bruise him. Yeah, she just might, but it still annoyed him that she had to be so careful.

Fuck cancer. Seriously.

"Now, sit down and stop being weird." She gave him a wink, and he sat down on one end of the couch, Tessa on the other. Brent sat on the armchair nearest her and leaned close.

This wasn't awkward at all.

"So, you work with your brothers, right?" Brent asked, and Murphy nodded.

"Yeah. My title is Lead Architect, but I also do some of the heavy lifting since we're a small company."

"A good one from what I hear," Brent added.

"Good to know we have a reputation," Murphy said easily. He blew out a breath and figured, what the hell, Brent seemed like a nice guy. "So, it turns out, in addition to all the other shit going on, I might be homeless soon."

"What the fuck?" Tessa asked, and Brent leaned closer.

Murphy told them about his lease and landlords and shook his head while he did it; more annoyed with himself now than ever before. He should have been asking to see his new lease long before this, but he'd been so used to how things had worked in the past, he'd been lazy. Not to mention between the extra projects at work and his diagnosis, he'd had other things on his mind. Now he was stuck, and he had no idea what to do.

"Well, damn," Tessa mumbled. "And you can't stay with your brothers. Not when they'll smother you. I mean, we all remember what happened to Owen when he got in his accident."

Murphy's gut clenched at the reminder of Owen's near-death experience, and he nodded. "Plus, I have to be careful with germs."

"I didn't even think of that." She blew out a breath.

"Would you be able to live with someone who is near other sick people? I mean, like someone who works at a hospital?" Brent asked, his face thoughtful. He hadn't asked *why* Murphy couldn't be near germs, and he wasn't sure the other man even knew since Tessa probably wouldn't have told him. Brent just seemed like a guy who rolled with whatever was going on around him and didn't ask a lot of questions.

Murphy nodded slowly, a little confused. "I'm not going to be able to avoid everything, but I really don't want to bog down my family's lives when they have so many new changes coming up, you know?"

"You should move in with Tessa then," Brent said, his voice sure and confident.

"What?" Tessa and Murphy asked at the same time.

Brent shrugged. "It's the perfect solution. He'll be near Owen and the others for whatever he's going through." He held up his hand as if to ward off comments. "I don't know what it is, and it's not my business. But it seems like, from what I'm gathering, you might need family. And Tessa has the extra space. Plus, I figured without Liz paying half the mortgage, she probably needs help there, too."

Murphy blinked before giving Tessa a cautious look. Her mouth kept opening and closing, and her right eye twitched. He had no freaking clue what that meant.

"Uh...that's an idea..." Murphy's voice trailed off. Had he somehow found himself in the middle of the *Twilight Zone*?

Was this guy really offering up his girlfriend's—or at least the woman he was seeing—house for Murphy to crash at? Did he really not care that Murphy would be living with his girl?

Okay, dude, that made no freaking sense.

If Tessa were with Murphy, and she definitely wasn't, he wasn't sure he'd be okay with another man living with her. Call him a caveman, but whatever.

Tessa seemed to shake herself out of her thoughts and then nodded. "It is." She cleared her throat. "It's a good idea." She gave Murphy a look he couldn't recognize. "No, really. You should. I mean, I have the room, and we get along. You need the space, and I promise not to hover like crazy. It's the perfect solution."

It was a goddamn insane solution. But it was the only one he had at the moment, and for some reason, instead of thinking about it, he did something monumentally stupid.

"Okay. Yeah. Let's do this, roomie."

He was an idiot.

4

No one had ever said Tessa made the best decisions, and today was no different. She'd actually agreed with Brent's idea, and now today was moving day for Murphy freaking Gallagher. Why had she agreed to let the hottest guy she'd ever known move in with her?

Because she was an idiot, that's why. A big freaking idiot, who couldn't say no to those pretty Gallagher eyes of his.

Yes, she needed the money. Yes, Murphy needed a place to live. *Yes*, living with one of his relatives might get tricky since he was about to go through treatment. *Yes*, she and Murphy were friends so she should have offered herself. *Yes*, she'd had naked dreams about him and had even put her hand down her pants to rub one off while thinking of him going down on her.

Yes, all of those things were true.

And yet...and it was the last one that made this a truly horrible idea.

She'd never lived with a man before other than her adoptive father. Well, she might have lived with her birth father, but she didn't remember those times. He'd been in and out of rehab and her birth mom's bed so much that she didn't know if he'd ever been there when she was. That was all beside the point though, because she truly had no idea what she was doing.

She couldn't live with Murphy Gallagher and remain sane. She also couldn't kick him out, because while she had an attitude according to most people, she wasn't *that* much of a bitch.

But what if she wanted to walk naked around her home? She couldn't do that now with him walking around, as well —hopefully fully clothed.

Images of a naked and wet Murphy sauntering around her home—because if he was going to be naked, he was sure as hell going to be sweaty, too—filled her mind, and she quickly pushed those thoughts out of her head. So what if Blake had told her that she'd been the one to pierce Murphy's dick. That, in fact, *all* of the Gallagher men had piercings adorning their most likely beautiful, long, and thick cocks.

That wasn't something she was going to think about.

She was surely *not* going to imagine herself accidentally going into the wrong bed and spooning him. Because, hello, she'd never *accidentally* gone into Liz's bed and done that.

Though she was pretty sure one of her exes had imagined that. Often.

Murphy was just going to stay with her until they figured out the next step of the plan. He would be her roommate.

And for fuck's sake, she had Brent. Brent. The sweet man who had offered up her home for Murphy as if he didn't care that she'd be living with the sexiest man on the planet.

So, apparently, Tessa was officially the worst person in the world.

She didn't like Murphy like that. He was hot, smart, and a wonderful guy, but he was her friend. She didn't *want* to have a relationship with him beyond what she had. What she wanted was to see how things went with Brent, the man she was currently dating, though they weren't at the boyfriend/girlfriend stage.

Because her life wasn't complicated enough.

"Move out of the way, heifer," Blake said with a laugh as she hip-checked Tessa out of the doorway. For a pregnant woman, Blake could sure move; though Tessa was pretty sure that box had been labeled *pillows*. That was a good thing because if Blake or Liz carried anything heavier than that, there would be hell to pay.

Tessa flipped her friend off with a laugh before going out to the moving truck for another box. Since everything was so last-minute, they hadn't been able to hire movers. Instead, Owen had done what he did best and arranged the family so they took shifts packing up Murphy's things, then sending the furniture and other items to their storage shed at their property, before transporting the things Murphy would need to her house.

Or *their* house rather.

She still owned it since the paperwork had gone through to get Liz off the deed, but Murphy would be paying rent and half the utilities. She hated having to charge him at all, but he'd insisted, and frankly, she needed the money to help pay for all the fees and the increase in her monthly bills now that Liz was gone.

She wasn't sure what would happen once Murphy was able to move out, but she didn't have time to think about it right then. First, she needed to find a way to make this whole roommate thing work.

"You sure you're able to do this?" Liz asked as she walked beside Tessa, a light box in her hands. "I mean, you didn't really sign up for a roommate."

Tessa put on her brightest smile and rolled her eyes. "I'll be fine. It's Murphy. He's a good guy, and I'm going to be completely safe around him."

"That's not what I meant, and you know it. I've seen the way you two flirt with each other. I used to think the two of you didn't mean anything by it, but now, I'm not so sure."

Tessa frowned, honestly confused. "He's hot, I get that. Hell, all the Gallagher brothers are, but that doesn't mean I'm going to jump him. I like him as a friend, and that's all I want. And though I'm sort of dating Brent, I don't do relationships. You know that. And even if I wanted to, it wouldn't be with Murphy. I wouldn't want to hurt what we have or ruin the dynamic of the group. And he'll be thinking of more important things in his life than wanting to jump me."

Liz studied her face before giving her a slight nod. "I want to believe that. But, Tessa, I don't want either of you hurt. I might be marrying into the Gallagher family, but you're still my family, too. We're sisters in everything but blood, and always will be, no matter how big of a family I marry into."

Tessa's heart ached at the mention of family, but she blew out a breath and waved it off. She didn't have time to go down that particular memory lane today. "We're not going to get hurt. Murphy is going to need a support system and a place to live while he's going through this, and between all of us, we can make that happen. He's just sleeping in your old room. Nothing is going to change."

That was a total lie, but Liz let her tell it.

"Two ladies in my bedroom, I'm one lucky man," Murphy said with a grin as he set down a box.

"That's the mother of my future child you're talking about," Owen warned. "Watch it."

Murphy's eyes widened. "Tessa? Why didn't you tell me?"

Tessa gave him a frown and put her hand over her belly. "I thought we were keeping it a secret, Owen."

"I've always wanted a sister wife," Liz added, her hand

over her own belly bump—only hers was real. "I'm just not sure on the sleeping arrangements. Should I spoon Tessa while you spoon me? Who gets to be the big spoon?"

"It's fun trying out being every spoon," Jake said. As he was part of a triad himself, he would know. "Believe me." He waggled his brows, and Tessa bit her lip so she wouldn't giggle.

Owen looked between Liz and Tessa, worry on his face, and Tessa broke out into laughter. The rest of them joined in as Owen rubbed a hand over his jaw.

"I swear to God, if our little girl ends up like her aunt Tessa, we're making her join a convent."

Murphy met Tessa's gaze as they both smiled widely. "You're having a girl?" Tessa asked, bouncing on her feet.

Liz shook her head. "We don't know yet. Soon, though, I think. Owen and I thought for like thirty seconds we'd want it to be a surprise, but we like our lists."

"Just don't do a gender reveal party, okay?" Tessa rolled her eyes. "I mean, the whole 'rifles or ruffles' thing is a bit much."

"No problem there. That whole thing freaks me out a little," Owen agreed. "Anyway, we're all done unpacking the truck, do you want us to help with the boxes in here?"

Murphy shook his head. "You made sure everything was labeled to the point of color-coding, even in such a short time. I can handle it from here. Go do what you need to for the rest of the day. Rowan's with her friends, but Noah is with your brother, right?"

Maya nodded. "Tabby and Alex are practicing with all the Montgomery babies for when they're ready to have kids. It makes it easy to find a babysitter for sure." As Maya had seven siblings and countless cousins, finding a babysitter wouldn't be a problem for her.

Tessa, on the other hand, only had her parents, and though they were amazing people, she still felt a little cut off from them. Her fault, she knew. She hadn't been an easy child and an even worse teenager. They'd never blamed her for acting out, but she sure as hell blamed herself.

"Tessa? You okay with me ordering a pizza?"

She blinked at Murphy's question and shook her head as she looked around the room, noticing that they were alone now. Apparently, when she'd been in her own little world, the others had left. Had she even said goodbye? Hell, she needed to get her head on straight—especially since this was Murphy's first night staying at the house, and she didn't want him to think she was a complete head case.

"No on the pizza? You okay, Tessa?"

"Sorry, yes, pizza is fine. I was thinking about something and, apparently, lost all track of where I was and how to act like a nice host. Did everyone leave while I was standing there drooling?"

Murphy chuckled and wrapped his arm around her shoulders while leading her back to the kitchen. "You weren't drooling. Much." He winked, and she punched him in the side before remembering that he was sick. She quickly pulled away and cursed.

"I am so sorry."

Murphy's eyes darkened. "You didn't hurt me. Don't treat me any different than you normally would. Okay?"

"I can't make that promise, but I'll try. And while we're making promises, don't hide your symptoms from me." He opened his mouth to say something, but she headed him off. "I know you're going to try and be tough and strong in front of your family, and I get that. You don't want them to worry. But, eventually, you're going to need to let things come out so you can heal. If you have to hide what's going on where you live, as well, it's going to just be tougher on you. So, never feel like you have to hide things from me."

She hadn't meant to say all that, but now that it was out, she knew it was exactly what she needed to say.

Murphy searched her face before nodding. "I'll try."

She cleared her throat, awkwardness settling between them. "Pizza?"

He nodded quickly as if thankful for the change in subject. She certainly was. "Pizza."

Once again, she hoped she knew what she was doing.

"I'M TOTALLY TEAM BUCKY," Tessa said as she leaned back on the couch. She patted her stomach, now bursting to the brim with pizza, soda, and ice cream. She hadn't eaten like this in months—if not years—and knew she'd probably regret it in the morning, but she didn't care. Not when they were celebrating Murphy's first night in the house.

"I don't think there *is* a Team Bucky," Murphy said from her side. He was also leaning on the couch but toward her so their shoulders pressed together. She figured they were both far too full and tired from moving his stuff in to move. "There's Team Captain or Team Iron Man. And I have to say, I'm going with Captain here. Tony is a misogynistic hypocrite. I mean, come on. He's the one who started the whole mess in the first place by being a selfish twat, then suddenly he changes his mind and actually has a real feeling about something, and now he wants everyone to follow the rules? Bullshit. He loves breaking rules. It's his thing."

She grinned and turned her head to look at him. His beard was a bit fuller than usual, and his eyes were droopy. She figured one of them would pass out soon from all the carbs and work they'd done, and she just hoped it wasn't on her couch. There was no way she wanted to wake up cuddling this man. Not only would it be a bad idea, but it would also feel too much like cheating on Brent. Sure, she and Brent were allowed to date other people, but Murphy would not be one of them.

"Still Team Bucky."

"Still not a thing."

"It totally is. I mean, I love Cap, but Bucky is where it's at. He didn't have a choice in anything that was done to him, and yet he's still fighting all that mind control and his past to try and find out who he is without Hydra. And if he and

Cap were together?" She closed her eyes and moaned loudly.

Murphy barked a laugh and nudged her thigh with his fist. "Actually, I can see that. Would be kind of hot."

Tessa opened her eyes and stared at him. "See? Team Bucky."

"You're insane. But I like you anyway."

"That's what they all say." They continued the movie, laughing and slowly getting a little more tired as the night went on when her phone buzzed on the table.

Murphy sat up with her to pause the epic final battle, and Tessa lifted her phone to see who could be calling after nine.

"Ah, yes, Dull Brent. How is Dull Brent these days?" Murphy's eyes danced as he said it, so she flipped him off. She didn't really mean it since she'd been the one to call Brent boring in the first place.

God, she was such a bitch sometimes. She answered the phone and stood up, waving Murphy off when he shook the remote. "Hey, Brent, we were just watching a movie. Let me get back to the bedroom, okay?"

"No problem. I just wanted to hear your voice before bed." She frowned at his words. He'd never said anything like that before, and she had to wonder if it was because Murphy was staying at her house or that maybe Brent was starting to feel more for her than she'd realized.

But, Tessa reminded herself, she'd made a promise to

try and make this relationship work so she would just attempt to stop overthinking things.

"I'll clean up," Murphy said quietly. "Night, Tessa."

She gave him a small smile. "Thanks, and good night, Murph."

He gave her a wink and went about cleaning up the rest of their mess, though they'd done most it before, as she walked back to her bedroom to talk to Brent. It felt weird being in the same house with Murphy alone after dark, but she knew she'd just have to get used to it. In fact, she'd have to get used to a lot of things.

Murphy was going to need her soon, even if he didn't want to, and she'd have to be the strong one—something she wasn't positive she'd been before, even though she'd tried. She blew out a breath, knowing there was nothing she could do for him now. Instead, she needed to focus on something she *could* get a handle on.

"So, you wanted to hear my voice?"

Brent was a good guy. He was a *nice* guy. And maybe if she tried hard enough, she could be the type of woman who would be good enough for him.

Maybe.

5

Murphy was going to throw up, and he hadn't even sat in the damn chair yet. Sweat broke out over his brow, and his palms went damp. *I can do this*, he reminded himself. It was just the first day, and he'd done first days before. And these treatments wouldn't even be as bad as the ones when he was a kid.

He only had to take a pill and then get blood transfusions since the components of his blood weren't doing what they should. He had to be on every supplement he could think of, as well, meaning his bedside table had bottles and bottles of vitamins that he put in those little weekly containers so he didn't forget anything.

It wasn't like before.

But it still sucked.

"You need to sit down?" Graham asked, his voice low. "I

mean, I'm having flashbacks here, and I wasn't even with you for most of the treatments."

Murphy blew out a breath and shook his head. "I'm fine. Really. Just a little freaked out, but you can't really blame me."

"Hell, *I'm* freaked out." Graham ran a hand over his big beard and sighed. "And Blake told me I probably shouldn't say things like that in front of you right away, but hell, I'm not good at this sort of thing."

Murphy gave his eldest brother a look. "Uh, that's where you're wrong. You excel at doing this sort of thing. You're always there for us no matter what." And given all the shit Graham had gone through before he met Blake, that was saying something.

Graham reached out and squeezed Murphy's shoulder, though not as hard as he normally would have. The fact that everyone continued to change their mannerisms so as not to hurt him made him feel cared for and annoyed all at the same time. It wasn't their fault that he had cancer, just like it wasn't their fault that they were doing their best to not hurt him because he bruised so easily now, but he still didn't like the constant reminder that he was sick. He didn't like that since they continued to change the way they interacted with him, they must always have the idea that he was sick in the forefront of their minds. And because of everything swirling his brain into a vortex of anger and self-pity, he just wanted to scream or hit something.

Not that he would, though. He had to be tough.

Showing weakness even when your body was actually weakening would only bring pity, and he wanted nothing to do with that.

"Let's do this," Murphy said under his breath.

Liz was already waiting for them near the front desk, her eyes going straight to Murphy's as they walked in.

"You're early, I like that." She smiled as she said it, and Murphy's stomach rolled.

Just get through this. It's just Day One. You can do it.

"I figured the party couldn't start without me so..."

She smiled again and lifted up a chart. "I need you to fill out some paperwork, and then I'll get your nurse to show you into the back area where you'll start your treatment. We're going to do a blood transfusion today as well according to Dr. Wilder."

He nodded and took the clipboard from her hand. "Got it." The transfusions gave him energy since it was literally replacing his weakened blood, so he didn't mind that part. It was the side effects from the pill that worried him.

"I won't be your nurse, though we already discussed that." Liz reached out and squeezed his hand. "I just wanted to be the first to see you." She looked over at Graham. "Since it's a shared room where there are going to be multiple patients getting their relative treatments, there really isn't a place for you to sit. I can get you a folding chair, or you can stay out here and wait."

Murphy glanced at Graham. "I could have driven myself, you know."

Graham narrowed his eyes. "And you might want to do that with your next few treatments, but not today. Not for the first one." What was left unsaid was the fact that their parents had been with Murphy for every single appointment. There was no way he would let his brothers and their families exhaust themselves because of him.

"Thanks." He sighed. "Seriously."

"I know." Graham lifted his chin at Liz. "I'll wait out in the waiting room since I'll probably break one of those chairs." He looked at Murphy. "You need me in there for anything, I'll be right by your side. Got me?"

"I got you. Thanks." He punched his brother lightly on the shoulder, then closed his eyes, and Graham brought him in for a hug.

"You've got this," Graham whispered, echoing Murphy's thoughts. "Fuck cancer."

Murphy pulled back and opened his eyes. "Fuck cancer," he muttered under his breath. And with that motto, he followed his nurse who had come to stand by Liz to the treatment room.

The room held ten chairs all hooked up to sensors and had IV stands attached to them. They looked like robotic recliners, though not as comfortable. Since it was still early, there were only a couple of people in the chairs getting their treatments. Some meds took only an hour to be delivered, while others could take over ten hours on a slow drip since adding IVIG or poison to your body wasn't the easiest thing in the world. Most people also had a bag of fluid attached since many meds couldn't be administered without it. Murphy would only be getting a blood bag that day through an IV, but he'd spent many days of his childhood with tubes in each arm and a port in his chest. Luckily—if he *could* be lucky about this—he didn't need a port as of yet. Since the chemo he was taking was in pill form to be administered over a couple of weeks, he had it easy.

Not that there was anything truly easy about cancer.

His nurse sat him down on a chair next to one of the other patients and started taking his vitals. She seemed like a nice woman, but she was quiet and worked quickly. Murphy didn't mind since that meant he didn't have to come up with small talk. He had his phone and tablet with him, and since they were going to use his left arm and thankfully not put the IV directly in the crook of his elbow, he could move around a little more freely than he would otherwise.

"Murphy? Murphy Gallagher?"

Murphy turned to see a face he hadn't thought of in years and broke out into a smile. "Max? Seriously? How the hell are you?" He winced and looked up at the multiple bags attached to his childhood friend's IV. "Uh, well, maybe I should have started with something different."

Max had been in the same treatment center as Murphy for most of their childhood. In fact, when Murphy's cancer had returned, so had Max's. They'd even had the same form of juvenile Leukemia and had been on pretty much the same schedule. Their parents had become friends between the hospital stays and doctor visits, but everyone had lost touch after both the teens had gone into remission. Life had gotten in the way, and Murphy was pretty sure none of them had truly wanted to continue thinking about how they'd met and become friends.

But here they were, together once again.

Seriously. Fuck cancer.

Max just shook his head and smiled. He'd lost his hair from what Murphy could tell, and had even lost his eyebrows and lashes. God, that had sucked when he was a kid, and it looked like it sucked just as much now.

"I'd say it's good to see you, but hell, man, we weren't supposed to come back here, you know?" Max reached around his IV tubes and held out his hand. "Hell of a long time, man. And I was actually okay with that, you know?"

Murphy shook Max's hand and nodded. "Why couldn't we have met over a beer or something?"

"Because, apparently, we're cancer buddies, and God has a sick sense of humor," Max answered dryly. "So, what are you in for this time."

"CLL. You?"

"Same thing as before."

Murphy held back a wince. Their form of cancer in adults was usually worse than in children.

"Don't look like that, man. I'm good. We're going to beat this thing, and are already well on our way."

Murphy winced. "It just sucks that this is our third time in these chairs."

"Tell me about it," Max mumbled, but his eyes were still bright. "But we'll get through it. We always do."

The nurse came back and fiddled with the IV bags before inserting the needle into Murphy's skin. She did it so quickly, he didn't even feel the pinch.

"Hey, not bad," Murphy said with a sad smile. "You're pretty good at this."

"You've got good veins, what can I say," Mona, his nurse, said with a sad smile of her own. "And I've been doing this for a while. So we're going to start you on fluids since that's what we love to do here, and then we'll get going. Try not to move your arm around too much."

"Understood."

"And here's your pill. I want you to swallow it for me and let me know if you feel any differently throughout your time here, okay? Dr. Wilder already went through everything with you, but if you have any questions, I'm here for you."

Knowing if he didn't get it over with, he'd just make the day grow longer, he swallowed the coated pill and drank a whole bottle of water. She studied his face before going to help another patient that had walked in when he and Max had been talking.

"So, how's life been?" Max asked once Murphy was settled. "It's been what, ten years since we last saw each other."

Murphy frowned but nodded. "About that long, I think. And things have been good up until this." He pointed down at the IV in his arm. "I own a restoration and construction company with my brothers, and we're doing pretty good there."

"I remember you saying that your brothers were thinking about opening one up when you were in high school. Glad to know they waited until you were old enough."

"Had to get experience first. We all went to school to make sure we could actually run a business instead of running it into the ground." It had been a close call as it was when they'd first started, but they'd eventually figured it out. Murphy just hoped his illness wouldn't set them back. He never wanted to be the weak link in the chain, but once again, it looked like he would end up in that role.

"Got yourself a wife yet?" Max added, leaning back in his chair. The man was still built, even though cancer had ravaged his body. He had more ink than Murphy, too, and would probably fit in with his brothers and his friends—the Montgomerys—easily.

"Not yet," Murphy said with a smile. "My brothers found theirs, but I'm still enjoying being a bachelor."

"Ah, that's what I used to think about myself. Then I met Abby." Max's smile was so bright, Murphy couldn't help but smile back.

"Yeah? How long have you two been married."

Max shook his head. "Not married yet. We've been together for five years or so now, but we're finally tying the knot as soon as I don't have to wear a hat to cover this bald head of mine. But now that we're expecting, I figure I might just have to let her convince me to move up the date."

"Congrats, man! When are you guys due?"

"Abby is five months along. So, yeah, we're getting there. Thankfully, we don't want a big wedding, you know?" He looked down at his IV and sighed. "No time like the present."

Murphy swallowed hard. "Yeah. I get that. So, two of my sisters-in-law are pregnant, and my other brother's wife just had a baby. I guess there must be something in the water."

Max smiled widely. "That's a bunch more Gallaghers out there. Better warn everybody."

Murphy flipped him off, and Max chuckled, shaking his head as an older man near them huffed. "Oops," Murphy whispered. Of course, it wasn't like this was the first time someone hadn't approved of what a Gallagher was doing in public. They were used to it by now.

"Are you starting trouble again?" Liz asked as she walked into the treatment room to check Max's vitals.

"It's what I do best," Murphy answered. "Hey, Max, I take it you know Liz, then?"

Max grinned up at Liz. "Yep. She's been my nurse since she started here a few weeks ago. Why?"

"She's marrying Owen." The world was sure damn small sometimes.

Max gave Liz's protruding belly a look and grinned. "Ah, the bearer of the newest Gallagher. I give you my sympathy." He winked as he said it, and Liz snorted.

"Either you two made fast friends, or you already know each other."

"We know each other from when we were kids." Murphy rubbed the back of his neck, feeling a little tired since he hadn't slept the night before and now had chemicals running through his body.

Liz gave him a sad look that she quickly masked, and he figured she understood exactly what he was saying. "If you need anything, you just let me know. Mona and I are here for the rest of the day."

Max nodded and leaned back, closing his eyes. His friend had paled a bit in the past few minutes and now looked exhausted.

"I'll let you nap," Murphy whispered. "It was good to catch up, though."

Max opened his eyes and smiled again. "Let's make sure to exchange numbers. I'm sure we'll see each other again, but I don't want to lose touch."

"I think that sounds like a plan." As Max fell asleep, Murphy picked up his phone, looking to see if he had any new messages. He didn't know what to think about the idea that Max was here with him. When he'd been in elementary school, he'd had two friends outside of his brothers. Max had been his cancer buddy, and another kid named Hugh had been his school friend. He'd ended up losing touch with both of them as he got older and had put them from his mind. When he thought about them back then, he immediately went back to that time when he was too young to understand fully what was going on but still so afraid of death he didn't know what questions to ask.

Now, he was older and right back where he started. He'd run from whom he was because he hadn't been sure who he could *be* when he wasn't sick.

Maybe it was time to find Hugh again and see how his old friend was doing. It had been years, and since he'd already seen Max and hadn't had a panic attack, maybe this would be good, too.

He looked down at his phone and grinned when he saw a message from Tessa. She'd sent a photo of their fridge filled to the brim with fruits, veggies, and meats, not a sugary or fatty food to be found.

Tessa: *No more carb loading for my roomie. Plus I don't want my ass to get fat. I think I'm still full after Team Bucky.*

Murphy shook his head and started typing back, careful not to jostle his IV.

Murphy: *Team Cap. And you didn't throw out the leftover pizza did you? I wanted that.*

Tessa: *Hell yeah I did. It was so hard that you couldn't get it in your mouth.*

Murphy pressed his lips together so he wouldn't laugh aloud.

Murphy: *You know that was too easy, don't you?*

Tessa: *Shut up.*

Tessa: *...*

Tessa: *Are you doing good? Graham and Liz taking care of you?*

Murphy: *Yeah...*

Tessa: *What is it?*

Murphy: *Just sucks, you know? But I'll be home soon hopefully and we'll just order the junk food in.*

It was weird calling her place home so easily, but Murphy didn't try to think too hard about that fact.

Tessa: *I'm making chicken tonight. No junk food Murphy Gallagher. Liz gave me a list.*

Murphy: *This is what happens when you have a nurse in the family. You lose all the good stuff.*

Tessa: *Are you saying my food isn't good?*

Murphy: *Uh...no?*

Tessa: *You'll pay for that. Now go get better and I'll be here when you get home.*

He grinned again before saying goodbye and setting his phone down on the small table next to his chair. This whole roommate thing was still a little weird, but she was making it pretty easy.

"Who has you smiling like that?" Max asked, pulling Murphy from his thoughts.

"Huh? Oh, just my roommate. She's throwing out all my junk food."

"She?" Max shook his head. "You don't smile like that for a roommate."

Murphy shifted in his seat, suddenly uncomfortable at where this conversation was heading. "Uh, I do. She's just a friend."

"Sure, Gallagher. That's what they all say."

Murphy frowned but didn't say anything back as Max fell asleep again. Tessa was just his friend and now his roommate. Nothing more, and nothing less. And now that he had this whole new set of complications in his life, he didn't need any more.

Thinking about Tessa Stone as anything more than his roommate would only lead to trouble.

Big trouble.

6

"Huh?" Tessa asked, truly confused. She'd had a horrible day at work where she'd wanted to quit more than once. Now, instead of heading home to curl into her couch and maybe even help Murphy if he needed it, she was standing in front of a café in downtown Denver, being dumped.

Like, what the fuck?

"You seem to be a wonderful person, Tessa, but it's just not working for me." Brent shifted from foot to foot, looking seriously stressed out and nervous. What did he have to be nervous about? It wasn't as if she would hit him for dumping her or anything, but it sure as hell looked as if he were ready to duck from an impending fist.

"And you couldn't have called me? You made me come all the way down here—after work, mind you—so you can say it's over? I mean..." So, apparently, she wasn't angry that he didn't want to be with her anymore, but more that she'd had to drive twenty minutes through traffic to be dumped. At least, she had her priorities straight.

BRENT LOOKED PAINED. "I didn't want to be rude, but I can see now that I went about this wrong." He ran a hand over his face, looking less put-together than she'd ever seen him. "I thought doing it face-to-face would work."

"Okay, then. Well, I'm sorry this didn't work out. I hope you find who you're looking for." There, she was civil. It wasn't as if she had been truly invested in the relationship anyway, and she figured that was part of the problem. She'd been stringing him along because she'd thought he might be good for her. But in the end, she'd been wrong.

"Uh...thanks. I guess I just couldn't deal with all the men in your life." He winced again. "Uh...I've got to go. Bye." He fled, leaving Tessa standing behind him like she'd just been slapped.

Men? What *men* were in her life? She didn't have any brothers, and she'd never introduced Brent to her family. Sure, she lived with Murphy now, but it had been Brent's idea in the first place.

She didn't have a man in her life. Brent had sort of been it.

Someone bumped into her from behind and kept going, practically knocking her to the ground. She couldn't see his or her face since they had their head down, and their hoodie up, but it didn't matter. Now she was just annoyed.

This week seriously sucked, and she wanted nothing to do with Brent or being out in the real world any more that night.

Screw Brent.

And screw thinking she could make a relationship work. She was better off with her hand and ice cream to make her feel better.

THE NEXT MORNING, she somehow found an empty parking meter off 16th St. Mall and filled it with as much change as she could find in her center console. She'd promised she'd meet up with Liz and the girls at a café called Taboo downtown. It was owned by one of Maya's friends, and even had a connecting door to Montgomery Ink, the tattoo shop that Maya owned with her brother, Austin.

Normally, Tessa wouldn't want to drive all the way downtown just for lunch on a weekend when there were plenty of good places near where they all lived, but since Maya had to work that day, it made sense. She did find it a little weird that she was starting to spend so much time with not only Maya but Blake, as well. But since Liz was marrying into the family, Tessa supposed this wasn't going to be a short-lived thing. At least Liz included her in her new life and these new connections. She could have put Tessa in her own separate bubble, and things could have still worked out. However, Tessa was starting to become friends with Blake and Maya on her own, and was coming to enjoy these lunches.

Of course, since all of them were now married or engaged to Gallaghers, it was still a little weird. She was living with a Gallagher but not actually seeing him. With the way meals and outings were evolving, Tessa and Murphy were constantly being thrown together in weird eighth and ninth-wheel situations that made things a little complicated. Or maybe it was just convoluted because she kept picturing Murphy naked.

She *really* needed to stop doing that.

Tessa had almost made it to the door of Taboo when she froze.

"It can't be," she whispered, her hands shaking. "It can't."

But it was. Her ex-boyfriend and the star of her recurring nightmares stood on the other side of the street, waiting at the crosswalk so he could come her way. She wasn't sure if he'd seen her, but she could damn well see him and wanted to find a place to hide. As hiding wasn't her style, that thought just made her even angrier.

How dare he be allowed to walk around as if he hadn't done what he did? As if he hadn't hurt her and made her feel like she was worthless. And the crux of it all was that she hadn't even noticed that he made her feel like crap until it was almost too late.

God, what was he *doing* here?

The light turned green, and he started to cross the street, so she ducked her head and quickly ran to Taboo, thankful that she had a place to go so she wouldn't have to face him.

He'd almost broken her once. But because there hadn't been any actual wrongdoing in the law's eyes, he'd been allowed to freely walk about as if he hadn't emotionally abused her...for years.

He'd hit her once, but that hadn't been enough for the police. They'd asked her what she'd done to cause him to slap her, and she'd walked out, not bothering to follow up on the assault charge. It wasn't as if they would do anything anyway.

She still regretted leaving the station as she had, but she couldn't do anything about it now. She hadn't seen her ex since that night, and had firmly put him out of her mind— or at least she had tried. Now, he was back in her thoughts and she couldn't quite keep her stomach from rolling.

"Hey, you okay?" Liz asked, coming toward her. "What's wrong?"

Tessa shook herself out of her thoughts, and gave her best friend a smile that she hoped reached her eyes. "I'm fine. Traffic, you know?"

Liz frowned, studying her face. "Uh-huh."

"Seriously. I had to parallel park and everything. But I'm good now, and in the mood for a huge salad." That much was true as Taboo had the best salads, soups, and sandwiches ever. The owner, Hailey, was a goddess when it came to food and drinks. If the woman ever opened up a full restaurant that served dinner, Tessa would probably gain twenty pounds from showing up every night.

"If you say so," Liz said, not sounding convinced at all. That's what happened when your best friend from college was *still* your best friend years later—you couldn't hide anything.

Tessa linked elbows with Liz and led her to the corner booth where Maya and Blake were already seated. "Hey, ladies."

"Hey, thanks for coming down here," Maya said as she scooted over. "It's just easier on a Saturday since we're so busy over at the shop."

Tessa sat down next to Maya as the two pregnant women sat in chairs across from them. Their bellies were starting to become a tighter fit, so Tessa didn't blame them.

"It's really okay, and I love the food."

"That's good to hear," Hailey said as she walked over to them. She grinned, and it only made her more beautiful. With her blunt blonde bob and killer eyes, that was saying something. "I have fresh peach tea in the back if you'd like that today, or I can get you something else to drink while you all decide what you want for lunch."

"Peach tea sounds amazing," Tessa answered honestly.

"Hey, what did I say about you waiting on us?" Blake said from her seat. "We're supposed to go up to the counter to order."

"You're my friends, so you're going to have to deal with me serving you here. So suck it." Hailey winked as she said it before heading back to the counter, and Tessa cracked up laughing. The other woman *so* did not look like those words would normally come out of her mouth, and Tessa loved it.

"So, do you want to tell me why you look like you've seen a ghost?" Liz asked, leaning forward so she could see Tessa's face better. Tessa had never been good at lying to her best friend, and today didn't seem like the day she'd suddenly start.

Maya tilted her head and studied her, as well, and Blake moved forward a bit so they were all staring at her, waiting for her to break. Or speak, whatever. It sure *felt* like breaking sometimes.

"I saw my ex outside," she said with a sigh. She didn't want to say his name as if saying it would bring him back into her life. She was superstitious that way. "He was walking across the street, and I sort of flailed my way in here.

Liz's eyes went wide while the other two women frowned. They didn't know what had happened with him, and this wasn't the place to get into it—if she told them at all.

"Are you okay?" Liz reached out and gripped her hand. Tessa gripped hers back before letting go so she could pretend she was relaxed.

"I'm fine. It just threw me for a loop." Oddly enough, Maya and Blake didn't ask for details like they normally would have, and Tessa was grateful for it. The women seemed to know that this was not a topic she particularly wanted to discuss now. Or ever.

"Do you need anything?" Liz asked, her voice low as Hailey came by with their drinks.

"I'm good." Or she would be. "And thank you," she said, smiling up at Hailey and hoping it looked genuine. It should be, considering she loved anything the other woman made, so she was truly excited about this peach iced tea and the massive salad she was about to order.

"You're welcome," Hailey said with a bright smile. "Okay, what can I get you guys?"

They ordered their food, making Tessa's stomach growl when before, she hadn't been sure she would be able to eat after seeing her ex. Hailey's food and being surrounded by friends that cared about her would do that.

"So, anything new going on?" Blake asked, rubbing her slight baby bump. "Rowan is hanging out with Graham today, working on a science project, so I'm free to listen to gossip." The other woman smiled. "I never used to have time for gossip."

Maya's eyes danced. "I always have time for gossip. It's sort of my thing."

"I would think with two men and a baby keeping you busy, you wouldn't have that much time," Tessa said dryly.

"Well, sometimes, Noah is sleeping, and it's Border and Jake's date night." Maya winked, and Tessa laughed with the others. How Maya could handle both Border and Jake, Tessa didn't know. But more power to her.

"Everyone take a moment to picture that," Blake said dramatically. They held a moment of silence. "And that's enough of that since we're in public, but really, anything going on?"

Liz shook her head. "Owen and I have just been working and trying to figure out when we're actually going to fit in a wedding while making the guest bedroom into the nursery."

"I'd bet you that Owen has a list of lists for that particular endeavor," Tessa said dryly.

"You wouldn't be wrong." Liz shook her head. "I think he's more prepared for this bundle of joy than I am, so while I'm stressed as hell about being a mother and actually giving birth, I know I can lean on him for things at home." Tessa ignored the slight twinge of envy at that. If anyone deserved this kind of happiness, it was Liz. "But as for the wedding? We honestly have no clue. I don't have many people to invite since I don't have a huge family." Liz winced. "Okay, so I have Tessa...and that's about it."

Tessa rolled her shoulders back, pissed off at the world once again for what it had done to Liz. "And I'm all you need, thank you very much."

"And you have the Gallaghers now," Blake put in.

"And the Montgomerys," Maya added. "I'd say if you want us, but first, why wouldn't you want us, and second, we don't really take no for an answer when it comes to invading your life. It's sort of our MO."

Liz wiped tears from her face, and Tessa moved to

squeeze next to her best friend in the booth. "I have no idea why I'm crying."

"Hormones." The three of them spoke at once, and that sent all of them into peals of laughter.

"Truth." Liz pulled out a tissue from her purse and wiped the rest of the tears from her face as one of Hailey's part-time workers came around with their food. The place had gotten busy as they talked, and Hailey was stuck behind the counter doing forty things at once as usual.

They spoke as they ate, talking about their weeks and what they had coming up. When it was Tessa's turn, she leaned back in her chair and frowned. "Brent broke up with me yesterday."

"Are you serious?" Liz asked, her eyes wide. "And you're just now telling us?"

"Are you okay?" Blake frowned and set her soup spoon down. "What happened?"

"I honestly have no idea. It was just weird, and it's not as if we were serious. Hell, we made it a point to make sure the other person knew we were allowed to date other people—even though I didn't. He might have for all I know." She ran a hand over her face, annoyed all over again with how everything had worked out with him.

"Did you really like him?" Maya asked.

"I think I could have. Maybe." Tessa let out a groan. "I think I *wanted* to. What kind of person does that make me?"

"Someone who was trying," Liz said firmly. "Did he say anything when he did it? Or was it by text or something?"

Tessa rolled her eyes, annoyed all over again. "He made me meet him in front of that café he likes a couple blocks from here. After work. Just to say it wasn't working." She let out a small growl. "And then he had the nerve to say I had too many men in my life or some crock like that. First, *he* was the one who said 'let's take this slow and casual.' Second, I wasn't dating anyone else."

Liz scowled. "You don't think he was talking about Murphy, do you?"

Tessa shook her head. "I don't know. Maybe? I mean, it was *his* idea for Murphy to move in with me. And I'm not *with* Murphy. We're just friends. Anyway, Brent made it sound like he was talking about more than just one man." She pressed her lips together, trying to calm her breathing. "It didn't make any sense, and yet somehow made me feel slutty."

"Well, fuck him then," Maya said simply. "He's an asshole. A boring asshole. If he's going to make you feel like a slut, then he can go fuck himself."

"Exactly." Blake raised her chin, her eyes blazing. "You two were casual and not ready to be serious yet. Even if you *were* dating twenty other men, so the fuck what? You never lied to him or kept things from him. Dull Brent can go jump off a bridge."

Tessa snorted. "I see you've been talking to Murphy with that nickname?"

"It stuck," Blake said with a shrug. "And I'm sorry he was a douche canoe."

Tessa grinned at the term, feeling better now that she'd talked it over with her friends. "That is true. I guess this means I can date one of those forty men he thinks I'm with."

The others laughed, and she joined in, knowing she needed to put Brent and her ex out of her mind. The only person she really wanted to talk to right then was Murphy so she could get his reaction to khakis-wearing Brent, but she refused to text him right then. He'd been sleeping when she finally got home the night before, exhausted from his treatment no doubt. And they hadn't really spoken that morning except to talk about grocery shopping. She'd tell him when she got home and see what he thought.

She refused to dwell on the fact that she was now planning her time, thinking about Murphy being in *her* home with her and how she truly wanted to talk to him. That would go down a dangerous road that neither of them should be on.

No matter how much her subconscious apparently wanted it.

7

"Hey, Murphy!"

Murphy looked over his shoulder from where he was talking to his friend and fellow architect, Storm, about an upcoming project and grinned.

"Hugh!" Murphy gave Storm a nod and went off to meet his friend. He'd looked up Hugh out of the blue after seeing Max at the clinic. He hadn't seen either of the men in years since they'd all aged and grown apart, but Murphy had wanted to change that. It might have been more out of curiosity than anything, but he didn't care.

His friend from school looked like he always had, just a few years older. Hugh wore dress pants and a button-down shirt, but since he wasn't working, he'd apparently left the tie and coat at home. Murphy thought of his worn jeans and T-shirt and mentally shrugged. He was who he was, and since he hadn't planned on meeting any clients today, he'd gone casual. Plus, he'd spent most of the morning with Storm, going through a hollowed-out bookstore that had been badly damaged during a fire. Storm's company, Montgomery Inc., was the one doing all the work, but Storm had called in Murphy for a consult. It was a big project, and the place belonged to Storm's fiancée, so Storm had wanted to be doubly sure on things before finishing up the plans.

Shaking himself from his random thoughts, Murphy walked up to Hugh and grinned. He was ready to give the other man a hug since he hadn't seen him in years, but when Hugh held out his hand, Murphy shook it instead. Apparently, not everyone was as casual with hugs as the Gallaghers. Sometimes, he forgot that.

"Good to see you, man," Murphy said after they had shaken hands.

Hugh grinned and nodded. "Good to see you, as well." The other man looked around the burnt building and grimaced. "Looks like something did a number on this place."

Since they were standing on the street instead of inside the building where Hugh could see worst of the damage, Murphy just nodded. There were too many safety concerns for Murphy to show his old friend around.

"Huge fire," Murphy confirmed. "Most of the bones are still intact, but it's going to take a bit for them to get things back to rights."

"Them?" Hugh asked.

"The company working on the project. They just called

me in to consult." He didn't mention that they were also related through Jake since Storm was Maya's brother. That just tended to confuse people. "I figured we could meet down here and get something to drink at Taboo." Murphy tilted his chin toward the café he and his family liked that was located across the street.

Hugh winced and looked down at his watch. "I can't really stay for coffee. I had a last-minute meeting pop up down here, so I figured I could stop by and chat for a bit before I go do that. Sorry."

Murphy shrugged, trying not to feel a little weird by Hugh's reluctance to stay for even a few minutes. After all, they hadn't seen each other in years. Murphy's email *had* been out of the blue, but if Hugh hadn't wanted to meet up, then Murphy didn't know why he'd agreed in the first place.

"No worries, I get it. I'm just glad you could come and meet up, even for a few minutes."

Hugh smiled, but it looked a bit off; as if he had something else going on in his mind that had nothing to do with Murphy. It made total sense, but it was still awkward as hell.

"Anyway, you look good, man. Life has been treating you right." Hugh's smile went a bit wider, and Murphy held back his own wince. He hadn't mentioned the fact that he was sick to Hugh as it really wasn't anyone's business, and now things just felt even more off.

"You, too," Murphy said instead. "Work doing well, then?"

Hugh nodded. "Tremendously. It's a casual meeting, or

I'd be a little more dressed up, but I figured it's okay to dress down once in a while."

Murphy pointedly didn't look down at his shirt from a local brewery. "I get it."

Hugh narrowed his eyes at Murphy's face, and Murphy could swear that there was something else going on here that he couldn't quite place. It felt as if there were animosity between them, and yet he had no idea where it could be coming from. Maybe he was just projecting. Or maybe the chemo was already messing with his brain.

"Anyway, I need to get going. It was good to see you." Hugh held out his hand again, and Murphy took it.

"Likewise." Well, didn't he sound like a pompous ass, but he wasn't sure what the hell was going on here.

Hugh left without another word and walked down the street in the direction he'd come from. Oddly, the man gave a backward glance toward Taboo, seemed to pause a moment, then kept going. Murphy had no idea what that was about, but he was a little too tired to care. Since Graham was working on Rowan's science project today and not able to make it in, Murphy still had to meet with Owen regarding an upcoming project down at the office. Jake would have come in as well to help now that he was taking a more active role in the company, but, apparently, he and Border had a day planned with Noah since Maya was working.

"Everything go okay with your buddy?" Storm asked as he walked toward him. "He didn't stay long."

Murphy shrugged. "He had other things to do. Anyway, do you need me for anything else today? I want to head to the office to see what Owen wants before I go home."

Storm reached out and gripped Murphy's shoulder. "No problem, man. Just take it easy, okay?"

Murphy sighed but nodded. "I don't plan on wearing myself out, but I'm not the kind of guy who just sits back and watches TV all day, you know?"

"Nothing wrong with that some days," Storm said with a grin. "Hell, I'm just now back on my feet from being laid up for weeks."

Murphy held back a wince at that since the other man had been injured pretty badly. But now, he was back on his feet—literally—and everything seemed to be going okay. Murphy was determined to make sure that outcome happened for him, as well.

"Good to see you working, though." He rubbed the back of his neck. "So, yeah, call me if you need me to look at anything for you along the way, but you've got this, man. Hell, you have way more experience than I do."

"Never hurts to use another set of eyes, just in case. Take it easy, man, and thanks."

"No problem." They said their goodbyes, and Murphy headed to his car parked behind his sister-in-law's tattoo shop since there was only one small spot behind the bookstore at the moment.

Feeling a little off after meeting with Hugh, he turned up the volume on his stereo and blared nineties alternative rock as he drove toward the Gallagher offices. Each jobsite had a small office as well that they used a lot, but when they weren't onsite and needed places to work, they had the main office. That was also where they met with clients more often than not.

Murphy had a slight headache, but unlike most people, he couldn't just take an aspirin and call it a day. So many things could interfere with his meds and cause side effects he really wasn't prepared for, so he chugged some water and hoped he was just dehydrated. If it persisted, he'd call the clinic and see what he could take that day.

He pulled into the lot and got out of his car, a little more tired than he'd anticipated. He might not be able to stay at the office for as long as he wanted, but he'd deal with it later. Being sick meant he had to change plans often so he didn't make things worse.

When he walked into the building, he heard voices that didn't belong to anyone he knew and he held back a curse. Owen hadn't mentioned that anyone was coming in that afternoon. If he had, Murphy would have worn something other than what he had on. He was batting zero that day in terms of wearing something appropriate, apparently.

Owen walked out of his office and smiled. "Hey, Murph, we have a couple of guests today."

Murphy tried to keep the growl out of his voice. "I can hear that."

"Oh, we're so sorry for just walking right in without an

appointment, but when we called, and Owen said he was working with you today, we just had to come over and meet the two of you." A fiftyish or so woman with light blonde hair that didn't look dyed walked out beside a man around her age with light hair, as well. They had to be husband and wife from the loving looks they gave to one another after she'd spoken.

"Now, Grace, darling, let the man at least relax a bit before you accost him."

"Oh, shush, Chris. We're just so happy to meet some of Tessa's friends."

Murphy froze, blinking a few times before noticing Owen making wide arm movements behind the couple. As Murphy had no idea what Owen was trying to say, he ignored his brother.

"I take it you're Tessa's family?" Though the two of them looked nothing like Tessa at all. In fact, Murphy couldn't see a single feature that told him that these two were related to Tessa, but from the way their eyes warmed, he figured he'd hit the nail on the head.

"We're her family, yes." Grace smiled widely. "Our daughter's mentioned you Gallaghers a few times when talking about Liz, and we just had to meet you."

"Plus, we knew what company we wanted to come to when we were finally ready to remodel our home. It's best to work within the family, I always say." Chris grinned with pride, and Murphy felt a little off-kilter.

"Oh? Tessa didn't mention you guys were looking for a

company. That's great you came to us. We'll totally take care of you."

Grace came forward and patted his arm, her smile kind and her eyes shiny. "I know you will. Liz wouldn't ever marry into a family that wouldn't take care of their own and others. She's like our daughter, though I don't think she sees it that way." The other woman winked. "We'll wear her down, though."

"Grace," Chris chided, though he held the same soft smile as his wife. "The boys here don't need to know all of that."

Grace waved him off. "Of course, they do. Owen is marrying our Liz, and now we hear Murphy is living with our Tessa. They're family now, too."

Murphy froze. "Uh, ma'am, we're just roommates. We're not..." This wasn't awkward at all.

"Oh, we know." Grace waved him off. "We're just glad Tessa had the room to help you out since your landlord went a bit crazy." She winked. "Tessa brought it up during our last phone call since I wanted to know if I could help with the wedding."

Tessa hadn't really mentioned her parents much—or at all—and he wasn't sure why. They seemed so *nice*. He didn't know what was going on exactly since there was an undercurrent here he couldn't quite place, but he hoped he would figure it out soon so he didn't misstep.

"Anyway, we need to head out and meet with one of Chris's old colleagues. When you're ready for a real meeting, you just let us know, and we'll be here. It was wonderful finally meeting you, and I do hope we see you again soon." Grace's eyes widened. "Oh! I know. Tessa is coming to dinner in a few days so we can tell her all about the remodel since we wanted to keep it a surprise that we want to work with Gallagher Brothers Restoration. You should join her."

Red Alert! Red Alert!

The sirens from Star Trek blared in his mind, and he did his best not to run away in terror. "Um, maybe? Let me talk it over with Tessa."

"It's really no problem. We'd love to get to know Tessa's friends more." There was an odd pitch to her voice, and Grace blinked quickly before Chris wrapped his arm around her shoulders.

The older man cleared his throat. "Owen, thanks again for letting us see the building. And, Murphy, it was nice to meet you. I'm sure we'll all see each other soon." The couple walked out after waving and left Owen and Murphy alone in the foyer.

"What was that?" Murphy asked, his voice rough.

"That was Tessa's parents being Tessa's parents, apparently," Owen answered after a moment. "I don't know much, but from what Liz has told me, Tessa didn't get along with her parents when she was a teenager, but I don't think it was because of anything Chris and Grace did. I think it was just normal teenage things." Owen paused. "That and the whole adoption thing."

Murphy rounded on Owen. "What adoption thing?"

Owen's face drained of color. "Oh, fuck. I didn't know Tessa hadn't mentioned it. Damn it. Liz told me in confidence, and I just spilled something that wasn't my secret to tell. Don't tell Tessa you know, okay? She wouldn't want to know that we were talking about her behind her back."

Murphy ran a hand over his face. "Are you saying Tessa was adopted? I don't need to know the details, but I want to make sure I'm not thinking the wrong thing and make things worse."

Owen looked visibly pained. "Yes, but I don't know the details, and they're not mine to know anyway. All I *do* know is that because of that, and probably many other things, Tessa didn't always get along with her parents. Liz says that Grace and Chris have always been nice to her, and though she knows they want to be close to both her and Tessa, she's always stayed slightly removed for fear of how Tessa might react. I don't know what that means or why Tessa would feel that way, and it's not my business. But Grace and Chris want us to work on their house, and they know about us because of Liz and Tessa." Owen blew out a breath. "They're also loaded from what I've heard, and their house will be a huge project for us and good for the company. But I didn't want to truly agree until we all met. This might get complicated."

As they were Gallaghers; apparently, they lived for complications.

"I think I'm too tired to dive into all of that right now. I'll have to think about it later. But, Owen? Family's family, right? I mean, Tessa isn't any different now than before we knew about it." He wanted to be firm on that, just in case there was a misconception.

Owen raised his hands, palms out. "Of course. I mean, to *us* it shouldn't matter, but..."

"But if Tessa has issues because of it, they aren't any less real. Got it. And now, I'm going home because I can't focus, and frankly, I have a feeling if Tessa doesn't approve of this, then we're not doing the job anyway. I'm not going to hurt her just for a big project."

Owen shook his head. "You don't have to explain that to me. She's Liz's best friend, and that means she's family. We'll talk it out when the time comes, but if she feels weird about it, then we won't do it. Simple as that." But they both knew there wasn't anything simple about it.

Murphy didn't want to meddle in Tessa's business, nor did he want to hurt her. So he'd make sure she was really okay with him working with her parents before the company took the job. That's what friends did, after all.

He made his way home after saying goodbye to Owen and knew he probably needed a nap. His treatments this time weren't as bad as when he'd been a kid, but he wasn't at full strength. Of course, he was probably also tired since he'd spent most of the night tossing and turning over very vivid dreams that involved Tessa, a can of whipped cream, and her screaming his name.

Talk about awkward that morning.

As soon as he walked into the house, however, he knew something was wrong. Tessa sat on the couch, a pint of ice cream in her hand, and a spoon dangling out of her mouth. She turned when he closed the door behind him and sighed, letting the spoon fall into the pint.

"Hi." The word sounded so hollow, he didn't even bother waiting for her to invite him to the couch, he just went straight to her. He lifted her into his arms and set her on his lap so she could rest her head on his shoulder. Tired or not, he still had his strength, thank God.

"What happened?" He kissed her forehead, running his hands down her sides and back.

"Brent dumped me last night. I'd have told you when I got home, but you were sleeping. Oh, and I'm pretty sure Brent thought we were fucking and I was a slut. So, yeah. I hate him."

"That fucker. Want me to beat him up?" He squeezed her tightly before pulling the ice cream out of her hands so they didn't end up a sticky mess.

"No, I just want to forget him. And I'm not a slut."

Murphy let out a low growl and kissed her temple. "You're not a fucking slut. No man should ever make you feel less than you are because they're insecure. If they can't handle who you are, then they can go fuck themselves."

She let out a watery laugh and snuggled into him. He willed his dick not to get hard since she was sitting on his lap and felt *really* good, but he knew that was a lost cause. They would just have to ignore Little Murphy being happy at the close contact. It was a biological function, after all.

"I hate men."

Murphy sighed and held on. "I'd say not all men, but then I'd sound like a Twitter asshole."

She laughed again, but this time, he didn't hear tears. "You could never be a Twitter asshole." She paused. "Thanks for holding me. I didn't know I'd react this way. I didn't know that I liked him that much."

"It's not that you liked him, I don't think. He made you feel like shit, and now you're upset about it. Right?"

"Yeah. Stupid Brent."

"Dull Brent is gone. No more khaki pants and boring talks about finance."

"Did he ever talk to you about finance?" she asked, laughing.

"No, but it seems like something he'd talk about. That, and golf."

She snorted into his chest and sank into him as they talked about nothing important. Soon, her breath evened out, and Murphy reached for a throw blanket to put over them. He was just as tired, so realizing that she was warm and safe in his arms, he let himself drift off, knowing that this might be the most comfortable he'd ever been. And because he was just tired enough, he didn't let himself worry about what it all meant.

8

A couple of days later, Tessa woke up with a headache and the sudden urge to work out. There had to be something wrong with her if a run sounded like the best thing ever, but considering that she hadn't slept much for the past week or so, she wasn't sure where she'd find the energy. She figured endorphins could give her a boost. Or maybe she'd just collapse in a heap afterward and finally get some sleep.

And why couldn't she sleep?

Not because she was stressed about her job because she wasn't any more stressed than usual. Not because she had dinner with her family soon, because she actually loved her family and wanted to see them. Not even because she'd been dumped by Brent and had seen her ex on the same day.

No, it was all because of *him*.

Murphy Gallagher.

Her roommate.

Now the subject of every sex dream her subconscious could possibly think up.

She'd ridden him, lain under him, had him slide into her from behind. He'd licked up every inch of her pussy, devouring her in her dreams until she woke up coming with her hand between her legs and her panties dangling off one ankle. And just when she thought she'd had enough, she'd fantasized sucking him until he shouted her name, his voice hoarse, and his hands tangled in her hair.

Murphy Gallagher was going to kill her, and he didn't even know it.

She needed to get out of the house. Now.

So, she put on her sports bra and tried not to accidentally choke herself with it, found a pair of workout leggings that had an inspirational quote on the side, and pulled on a tank with a matching quote. She might not work out as much as she should, but she had kickass activewear for motivation. After sticking her ear buds into her ears and setting her jogging playlist to repeat since she sadly didn't have enough songs on it, she stretched and started her run.

Her lungs were going to kill her. She just knew they were inside her rib cage, holding on for dear life and screaming about how she was murdering them. But Tessa continued, telling herself that after half a mile or so, she might be able to catch her breath and not feel like she was dying with each step. At least that's what she vaguely remembered from her last time running.

Tessa wasn't the skinniest woman in the world, and she was just fine with that, but she still figured she should probably exercise more than once a week if she wanted to stay healthy. She just wished she could keep her weight steady by eating ice cream.

After the first mile, she could finally breathe again and started to remember why she liked running. It let her focus on what was around her at the same time it let her mind wander. And since she vehemently did not want to think of her roommate, she went through her checklist of things that should have been on her mind.

Roger Sanders, her co-worker and general pain in her behind, was starting to annoy her more every day, but she could usually tune him and his complaints out. As with any hospital in this economy, things were tightening up and getting more stressful by the month. Tessa had more patients than ever. And she had to wade through them all to ensure that they were not only paying but also not being scalped by the insurance companies. The latter was an ongoing, uphill battle, but Tessa refused to quit fighting for people's health.

She huffed out a breath as she climbed another hill and cursed herself for living in Denver instead of a completely flat place and at a lower elevation like Nebraska. At least she wasn't running on an actual mountain.

Her phone buzzed on her armband, and she looked down at the screen and smiled before answering.

"Hey, Liz." She panted between the words, and her friend laughed.

"Running? Really? It's super early, Tessa," her friend teased, but Liz was not wrong that running at this time of day was out of character for her. Hell, running outside was out of character for her these days.

"If it's so early, why are you calling? Is everything okay?" Tessa turned the corner and started down a new block so she would end up going downhill for the end of the run. She was already sweaty, and her joints ached, so hopefully she'd be able to sleep eventually.

Liz sighed, and Tessa went on alert. "I'm fine. I almost just walked the few feet that separates our houses to see if you wanted coffee or something, but then I remembered Murphy was there, and I didn't want to wake you. Hence the call. But I honestly didn't expect you to be running right now. How can you talk and run at the same time? I'd run out of breath."

She was not wrong. "You do most of the talking."

Liz laughed before letting out another sigh. "I have no idea how we're going to plan a wedding, Tessa. I mean, I just want to be married. I don't need tulle and lace."

"You might not need all of that, and honestly, I don't think Owen needs any of that either." Tessa coughed, out of breath but needing to reassure her friend. "Make it small. Intimate. Casual." Apparently, she only had enough energy

for one-word sentences. Why had she decided to run
so far?

"I want to tell him I love him and that I want him to be
mine forever just like I'll be his. I hope he already knows
that but..."

"You want it to be a ceremony." Tessa panted and wiped
sweat from her brow. She was officially a hot mess, and her
legs were going numb. *Almost there*, she thought. She could
see her house and would be able to shower before passing
out soon.

Thank God.

"I want to tell him I love him and make those promises
in front of our friends, but I don't want it to be a big deal."
Liz sighed into Tessa's ear, and Tessa almost passed her
house to get to her friend and give her a hug, but she was
honestly so sweaty, she'd just make Liz feel ill. She
promised herself she'd go over after she showered.

Tessa paced around her front lawn and started her cool
down so she wouldn't end up hurting herself. "Then make it
casual. You'll be fine, babe. Do it in our backyard and only
have *some* family show up like you wanted. Wear jeans if
you are feeling frisky."

Liz laughed, and Tessa felt a little better. "Owen's
already planned for that, and I need to stop freaking out. It's
just weird that he's a better planner than I am."

Tessa grinned as she opened her front door and walked
inside, toeing off her shoes since they were still a little damp
from the morning dew. "He's Owen. It's what he does. Okay,

I'm home and need a shower. After I'm all clean since...oh, my God, I'm sweaty right now, I can come over and have coffee with you. Sound good?"

"I need to head in to the clinic for a bit, or I would. I'm trying to get everything organized there for when I have the baby. I can't believe I'm going on maternity leave right after starting a new job."

"You're the best at what you do, Liz. Not even taking the legalities into consideration, they're lucky to have you. And I might come by the clinic anyway with some coffee just to see how you are. Even though it's my day off, I need to stop by the hospital later to look up a few things."

"And you called me a workaholic," her best friend teased.

"That's still true, and I never said I wasn't one. Okay, I'm off to shower. Now, go find your fiancé and make out with him a bit before you leave."

"As Owen just walked in wearing nothing but boxers and bed head, I can make that happen."

Tessa groaned and said her goodbyes, but she knew they fell on deaf ears as Liz let out a squeal at something Owen must have done as the call disconnected. The two of them were so in love it was sickening—in the best way possible. However, Tessa *really* didn't need to hear them having sex. Again. The walls in her house weren't all that thick, so she'd heard enough of Liz's begging, and Owen's deep voice in the throes of passion for a lifetime.

"Eek," Tessa mumbled and rolled her shoulders as she

closed her bedroom door behind her. She hadn't seen Murphy up and about, but he could still be sleeping since it *was* a bit early. Since Liz had hung up, Tessa's music was now blaring again in her ears, but she kept it on since she enjoyed the song. Wiggling her hips to the beat of the music, she stripped out of her sweaty clothes and stuck them in the hamper near her bathroom door. Naked, she closed her eyes and danced her way into the room, that endorphin burst hitting her just right. Maybe after her shower, she'd use her newfound energy and work on another project around the house after she stopped by the clinic to visit Liz. She still had a few things she wanted to upgrade since she'd really only just bought the house.

Her eyes still closed, she turned and smacked into a wall. Only, it wasn't a wall. It was a wet, hard, *very* male body.

Mortified, Tessa let out a scream, opened her eyes, and pulled out her ear buds. "Oh. My. God."

Murphy looked down at her, his wet hair dripping down over his eyes as he blinked, his mouth gaping. He'd gripped her upper arms when she'd slammed into him, so now he held her close, her breasts against his chest, her nipples pebbling into hard points and pressing into his wet skin. His cock hardened quickly between them, and Tessa felt the distinct coldness of the metal piercing on the tip pressing into her stomach. Somehow, her thighs had spread just enough when she ran into him for his thigh to press between her legs and right against her pussy. And since he was wet, hard, and oh so damn sexy, she could *feel* herself growing more aroused and knew she was just as wet as he was.

Holy. Fuck.

This was *mortifying*.

"Shit, shit," Murphy mumbled, shaking his head as if to clear his thoughts. He stepped back quickly, almost jarring her in the process, and reached for a towel. Since she only had the one extra large towel near them, he held that out to her and grabbed a freaking hand towel to cover himself with. Since the towel wasn't that large, and Murphy seemed to be growing by the second, nothing seemed to help.

Tessa pulled her gaze from his deliciously thick penis and looked right into his eyes as she wrapped the towel around her.

"What the hell? Why are you in my bathroom? Why are you *naked* and wet in my bathroom? Boundaries, Murphy! Boundaries!" She was rambling, and she didn't care. She'd just run five freaking miles to get him and his pretty dick out of her mind, and now she had a real image of said dick in her brain, and she'd never be able to think straight again.

Why did the Gallaghers have to be so sexy? Why did *this* particular Gallagher have to press all her buttons just right and happen to be naked and wet in her bathroom while she was sweaty and naked right in front of him?

The horror, Tessa thought. *The horror.*

Murphy winced and waved over at the sink where

another towel lay. She recognized this as one of Murphy's, so she threw it at him.

"Sorry, I didn't want to put it on the floor or on top of your towel so I left it over there."

"Still doesn't explain anything, Murphy Gallagher." She would never be able to get the sight or *feel* of him out of her head now.

"The showerhead in the guest bath broke off. I wasn't even touching it. When I went to turn on the water, it fell off and sprayed me in the face. The damn thing hit me on the hip on its way down." He pointed to a growing bruise on his side, and Tessa's eyes widened, panic leaping into her throat.

Without thinking, she reached forward and slid her fingers down his hip right above his towel. "Oh God, Murphy. Are you okay? You're bruising so quickly." She held back tears, annoyed with herself for showing weakness in front of the man who was actually going through this whole ordeal instead of just witnessing it.

He put his hand over hers, and she stilled, aware of what she was doing. Blushing once again, she pulled back and tightened her towel around her chest.

"I'll be fine. I'm headed into the clinic later anyway for my scheduled blood transfusion. That's why I needed to jump in your shower. I'm going to be late, and I didn't have the parts to fix the other one anyway. Since part of the showerhead is still on the wall, at least it's not spraying water everywhere unless I actually turn on the faucet, but

I'll have to shut off the water to the whole house once I start working on the plumbing. It won't be a hard job." Murphy blew out a breath and rubbed his face with his hand, keeping his other hand firmly on the towel around his waist. "I'm sorry for using your shower without asking, but you weren't here, and I figured I'd clean it before you got back. I didn't imagine you'd literally dance in naked and bump into me." He winced, but she saw something in his eyes that looked like interest.

God, this was all just a mess, and she didn't know what to do about it.

"It's okay," Tessa said slowly, trying to get images of Murphy and his pierced dick out of her brain. It wasn't easy since he was *still* naked and wet in front of her. "Really. We'll just forget this ever happened and go about our day. Why don't you, uh, go to your room and get dressed or something, and I'll shower and put this whole thing out of my mind." She spoke quickly and hoped he would agree to forget it all as she'd said. Not that she'd actually forget, but she could lie with the best of them. "Do you need me to, uh, go to the hardware store or something and pick up a new showerhead?"

Murphy shook his head. "I can do it. We have a few on-site that could work, and I can get them at cost to save money. I can even bring a couple home with me if you want so you can pick it out. It's your house, after all."

Right. It was her house, and he was her roommate. Her

naked roommate. She *really* needed to stop thinking about that.

"I don't know what I want for that bathroom yet, I haven't decided on anything. Liz was the one with the plans for the house."

His gaze softened. "No problem. I'll bring a couple by, and you can choose. If you don't like any, then we'll go to the store together to find one that you like that will also work in the space you have. Again, sorry for using your shower without asking, and for..." He waved between them.

"For slapping your naked body against mine so close I know exactly what your piecing feels like?" Tessa slapped her free hand against her mouth, her eyes going wide.

Murphy let out a rough chuckle that went straight between her legs. "Yes. That. Though we aren't thinking about that, right?"

Tessa nodded, her hand still over her mouth lest she make things worse.

"Right," he mumbled. "I'll just...I'll go." He fled the bathroom, careful not to accidentally brush her on his way by, and Tessa lowered her hand, closing her eyes so she could hide from the world and what had just happened.

This was what happened when you roomed with the guy from your sex dreams.

Bad things.

Bad, sweaty, naked, pierced *things*.

9

Murphy was pretty sure he'd end up with a strained groin soon if he didn't get his dick under control. It had been two hours since he'd had Tessa's sweaty, naked, curvy, and fucking *perfect* body pressed tightly against his, and he couldn't get the memory out of his mind.

Her breasts had been full, high, and tight, and more than enough to fill his large hands. Her nipples had been hard against his chest, and he'd almost sent out a shocked moan at the sensation once he realized exactly what had happened. Her hips had flared out, wide enough for him to hold onto as he pounded into her from behind. Of course, he'd noticed them right away since he'd always had a fixation on her hips, but he had gripped her upper arms rather than her delicious hips so he didn't do something stupid like bend her over. Of course, with his grip the way it had been, he could have easily lifted her onto his cock and fucked her hard against the wall. So, of course, he hadn't done that.

But then her thighs had spread ever so slightly, and his own thigh had slid between them, her pussy wet and ready on top of him. She'd been so hot, so damn *amazing,* that he'd almost come right then. He'd just about died and gone to heaven, and he'd only had the barest touch of her—in a situation that neither of them would have ever thought possible.

He both despised and loved his broken shower now, but he had a feeling there would be no going back after this. He'd try his best, but something had changed. He'd seen the interest in her eyes, and it wasn't the same as their usual flirting.

He just had no idea what to do, because when she'd mentioned his cock and his piercing, he'd almost burst... again. Sure, he was attracted to Tessa, but there was no way he should be wanting more than what they had. He couldn't continue to desire her like this and not make things weird for them. She'd opened up her home to him, and he wasn't about to jeopardize her graciousness or their friendship because he couldn't keep his dick under control with her around.

Murphy wasn't sure what he was going to do, but he knew he would have to do *something.* He wasn't sure he'd be able to be just friends, or sit there and watch her be who she was. Because Tessa was freaking amazing. She was caring, funny, sexy as hell...just a really deep person. Everything she did was either for someone else, or somehow geared towards helping other people.

And it didn't help that all he wanted to do was strip her down and make love to her until they were both exhausted. With everything else going on in his life, he knew doing anything to jeopardize their friendship would ruin everything that he had, and might even break him in the end.

"Are you okay over there?" Max's words brought Murphy out of his thoughts, and he shook his head, trying to keep a neutral expression on his face.

It wasn't working.

"I'm fine."

"You're not fine. There's something going on in that brain of yours. So, why don't you just tell me what it is, because we're going to be sitting here for a few hours. We might as well figure out how to make everything work. I mean, we've known each other for years. We may not have seen each other for a few of those years, but I know when you have something on your mind that you need to get out. So, why don't you just tell me, and we'll figure it out. It's a woman, isn't it?"

Murphy turned to look at his friend and winced. "It's a woman."

"It's always a woman." Max shook his head and reached out to lightly pat Murphy's free hand. Max had ink up and down his arms, and Murphy figured that he had tattoos down the rest of his body, too. Murphy had some ink, but not as much as Max. Somehow, the ink worked for both of them, and if Murphy, no, *when* Murphy got better, he knew he would have to get more. You only got tattoos when something was important in your life. At least, that was what Murphy figured. He would beat this. He would get healthy. No matter what.

Once again, Murphy shook his head, annoyed with himself for letting his thoughts go down that path. Here he was, ready to spill his guts about Tessa to his old friend, and yet he couldn't get the subject of his mortality out of his brain. There was seriously too much going on in his mind, and talking to Max would just have to help him. It had to.

"She's my roommate." Murphy sucked in a breath as soon as he got the words out and quickly looked around him, praying Liz hadn't heard. The fact that she worked here was usually great because he always had family around him, but it made it really difficult to talk about her best friend when he didn't want anyone to know about his feelings. Not that he exactly knew what his feelings were, but still.

Max smiled. "Your roommate? The hot one that's friends with your soon-to-be sister-in-law?"

Murphy took another quick look around. "Do you think you could speak any louder? I'm not sure the building next door heard you."

Max threw his head back and laughed. "Liz isn't around. She's not going to hear the fact that you might have a crush on her best friend, your roommate. Though, of course, the whole idea that you have the hots for your roommate is one of the best circumstances around, don't you think?"

"I never should have told you this." Murphy rubbed his free hand over his forehead, trying to stave off the upcoming headache he knew would be around any minute. He was already exhausted, and the blood transfusion hadn't given him any energy yet—it had just started. He had a feeling this whole conversation was going to end up giving him a migraine or an ulcer. But, of all people, telling Max was probably the best idea he had—not that it had been his idea in the first place. He couldn't tell his brothers or any of his friends who worked with the Montgomerys. Everyone was so interconnected, it would eventually get back to Tessa. He just knew it. And he wasn't ready for that. Hell, he didn't even know how he felt. How was he supposed to make sure she knew what he felt?

"Yes, you should have told me. Not that you actually told me anything." Max smiled again and sighed. "Why don't you just start from the beginning and tell me what's going on in your mind. Like I said, we have a while until we can get out of these chairs. We might as well make it interesting. And you know that healing takes every ounce of mental power and everything in our hearts to work. You can't be so stressed out about other things in your life that you forget to take care of yourself. So, tell me, what is it about Tessa that's leaving you in a hard place?"

Murphy winced at that description. "Maybe we shouldn't mention the word *hard* when it comes to Tessa."

Maxed cracked up laughing, and the other nurse on call walked in to make sure everything was okay. The two men brushed her off and said they were just joking around and promised not to disturb anyone else. While she thanked them, she said that seeing them laugh was worth any disruptions. Murphy figured there wasn't that much laughter in a room like this, and if telling Max about his feelings for Tessa brought a smile to his friend's face, then so be it.

"Tessa and I are just friends. We've only been friends. Sure, the two of us have flirted on and off—okay, mostly on —since we met, but that doesn't mean anything. We just like messing with each other. She's freaking hot, and frankly, just a kickass person. If she were anyone else and not best friends with Liz, I would have probably already slept with her. Maybe even be in a relationship with her that is something more. But that's not what happened, and she and I have been very careful to keep our flirting on a level we both could back down from easily."

"And now you're living with her," Max provided.

"And now, I'm living with her," Murphy mumbled. "I knew it would be weird to live with her. I mean, come on, I haven't lived with anyone since I lived with my family back in the day. And before me, Tessa only lived with her best friend. Hell, I don't even know if Tessa has ever lived with a man before. But despite that, I thought we were making it work. We were setting up boundaries and made sure we didn't cross them. Sure, there was still some casual flirting, but it wasn't like it used to be. We were making things work," he repeated.

"Then what happened to change all of that?" Max asked.

"Other than the fact that my dick is perpetually hard around her, and I can't sleep through the night because all I keep thinking about and dreaming about is her in bed with me. And not even just on the bed. Sometimes, we're in the shower. Or in the kitchen. In the car. Even on the couch. In my mind, I have crossed so many boundaries that I don't even know how I can look her straight in the face anymore."

"But you haven't actually crossed those, right? I mean, you haven't made her uncomfortable or acted on those thoughts?"

Murphy shook his head. "No, I've been good. Before this, she was dating some loser, so I was really careful not to make her feel weird. But now, that's over, and..."

He wasn't sure he could tell Max this part, but they were alone in the room and had quieted down enough that none of the nurses had come in to check on them.

"And?"

"And this morning, I saw her naked. *Felt* her naked. She saw me naked. Felt me naked. It was a whole lot of naked, and a whole lot of touching, and I don't even know what to think about it."

Murphy explained the events of that morning and everything that had been said. He even told Max about what Tessa had said about his piercing. It was way too much

information and pretty mortifying, but he had to tell someone. It wasn't like he could tell his brothers about something like that. Not when it came to Tessa anyway.

Max didn't laugh, nor did he shake his head and look
disappointed. Instead, the other man looked thoughtful.

"What?" Murphy asked, suddenly worried about what
his friend would say.

"Do you like her?" Max asked quietly. "And not just
because she's hot. But do you *like* her?"

"Yes," Murphy answered quickly, not even stopping to
think about his answer.

"We only live once, Murphy. You, above anyone, know
that. It's why we're here. Because no matter how many times
you want to reboot, how many times you want to start over,
we only live once. So, if you like her, and you can't stop
thinking about her, then maybe you should go for it. I'm not
saying make it all about sex or even make it a serious relationship. But you should talk with her. Because there's
something in your heart that's telling you that you need her
in some way. You might not know what it means exactly,
and she might not have the answers, but you deserve to find
out. Don't let life pass you by because you're scared of what
might happen if you take the chance. Not all of us are
blessed to live as long as we'd like. So take what you have,
live with what you have, and see if she is for you."

Murphy's stomach clenched at the reminder of exactly
why they were in these damn chairs to begin with. He
honestly didn't know what he was going to do about Tessa,

but he couldn't spend so much time and energy worrying in the dark over what could amount to nothing....and everything.

Before either of them could say anything else, however, a petite blonde woman with a tiny baby bump and a bright smile walked into the treatment room. Though Murphy had never seen her before, between the bright smiles on both her and Max's faces, he knew exactly who this woman was.

"Abby," Max breathed, reaching out for his fiancée.

"I know I said I'd be here later, but they said I was allowed to bring you lunch, and I wanted to eat with you rather than alone in the waiting room." She smiled again at Max before turning to Murphy. "And you must be Murphy. It's so nice to finally meet you after hearing such great things from Max."

Murphy chuckled. "Glad he only told you the good things."

She waved him off and grinned. "He's a great guy like that."

"Nice to meet you, too, Abby. Max has told me so many great things about you, as well." And he wasn't just lying to make her feel better. Max went on and on about how amazing Abby was and how much he was looking forward to their upcoming child and marriage. These two were seriously perfect for each other, and while Murphy could have felt a little jealous, he knew that no one deserved this more than Max. Maybe it was time for Murphy to figure out his own future. He'd spent so much time recently trying to figure out exactly who he was in a life where he had a future that he'd forgotten to *live* his present. Or maybe it wasn't as deep as all of that and he was just too much of a coward to do anything about Tessa.

Abby took a free chair next to Max, and the two of them talked quietly while eating their lunch. Murphy, meanwhile, leaned his head back and waited for his blood transfusion to be done. Thankfully, there weren't that many people in the clinic that morning, so Abby wouldn't have to sit on a folding chair, and Murphy wanted to give them as much privacy as possible since his treatment would be done far sooner than Max's.

"Murphy?"

He opened his eyes, unaware that he'd actually fallen asleep while waiting for his transfusion to be over. "Tessa?" He had to be dreaming because he had never seen her at the clinic before. She stood in front of him, two to-go cups of coffee in her hands, and a weary expression on her face.

"Hey. I came to drop off coffee for Liz since she and I talked this morning." She clamped her mouth shut at her words, and Murphy knew from the blush in her cheeks and the heat in his groin that they were both thinking about what else had happened that morning. Since this wasn't exactly the place or the time to talk about the shower incident, Murphy was grateful when she brushed right over that uncomfortable subject and continued her other train of thought. "Since I was here, I figured I should bring a decaf latte for you, as well. I noticed you have been drinking decaf instead of regular at the house, so I didn't know if that was just your favorite thing, or if you couldn't have caffeine right now. Either way, I have a regular and a decaf latte. I'll take whichever one you don't want. But I figured since I was here, I should bring something for you, too."

Murphy smiled and waved her over to the empty seat on the other side of him. "I'm trying to cut back on my caffeine while I'm on treatment, though I don't necessarily have to. So, thank you for the latte. I'm going to drink all of it right now." He winked, trying to bring everything back to normal. It wasn't easy, however, when she was so close that he could smell the peach scent of her shampoo and bodywash. Now *he* smelled like peaches, too, since he'd used her body wash that morning. He'd brought in his own shampoo but had forgotten soap. Now, every time he scented peaches, he was going to get hard.

It would be hell.

She smiled at him, and Murphy caught Max's wink out of the corner of his eye.

Yep, Murphy thought, *I am in trouble.*

10

Tessa was a mess. But considering she'd been a mess for far longer than just the time Murphy had lived with her, she couldn't totally blame it on him. She couldn't keep Murphy out of her brain, nor could she keep thoughts of work and her family off her mind. Everything jumbled together, and she could barely keep a straight thought. It was so exhausting.

She'd done a ten-hour shift that morning at the hospital and was now finally home. All she wanted to do was veg out in front of the television with junk food. Of course, that meant she would probably have to spend time with Murphy because he hadn't been going out as much as he used to— or at least as much as she thought he used to. In all honesty, she hadn't been going out as much as she used to in the past either. Considering she and Liz had met Owen and Murphy at a bar one night when Tessa had had too much to drink, her life had gotten a little more sedate since then. Most of her friends, okay her *only* friend, Liz, was now settled down, happily pregnant, and about to get married. As she really didn't like going out drinking alone, contrary to how she'd first met Murphy, she was stuck at home most nights. Not that she truly felt all that stuck anymore. She was now in her thirties. Maybe going out to bars every night wasn't exactly what she wanted to do. Sitting at home with Netflix was sometimes the best evening of all. But now she'd have to spend that time with Murphy because she wouldn't force him to spend all his time in his room.

Alone.

Naked.

Touching himself.

Oh, God.

Stop thinking that.

Stop it.

All that naked flesh. Those tattoos. Those *piercings.*

"Are you okay over there? Your face is really flushed."

Tessa looked up from where she'd been standing in the open fridge for who knew how long and coughed at Murphy's question.

"Uh, I'm fine. Just uh...I made Jell-O." *Oh, good, Tessa, now you sound like you're going off the deep end. Keep talking about Jell-O.*

Murphy raised one gorgeous brow and gave her a look. "You made Jell-O?"

She nodded. "Well, I was in the mood for shots. Or I

thought I was. Then I remembered that you really aren't drinking right now. So, instead of making Jell-O shots, I just made virgin Jell-O shots, which is really just Jell-O."

Murphy grinned and leaned against the wall next to her. "Really? You made virgin shots?"

Tessa winced. "And really not even that. Because I wasn't adding the tequila or vodka or any other alcohol to them, I didn't really feel like wasting my little cups, so I just made a batch of Jell-O."

He laughed and moved to stand by her, their shoulders brushing ever so slightly. Somehow, neither of them visibly reacted, but she *knew* he was just as nervous about tonight as she was.

It was their first night alone in the house after the *incident*. He'd spent the night before with his brothers after treatment before coming home when she'd been locked in her room, avoiding him. It had been less than forty-eight hours since she'd pressed her naked body against his equally naked form, and she had no idea what she was going to do about it. So, a sugar high it was.

"You made a bowl of Jell-O."

"Uh-huh. I figured if we really want to do sugar shots, then we'll just call them Jell-O spoons." She let out a groan. "It sounded cute in my head when I thought it. Now, it just sounds stupid, and I want to go hide under the covers."

Murphy wrapped his arm around her shoulders, and she tried not to lean into his hold. What was *wrong* with her? This was *Murphy*. She'd been around him long enough not to swoon like some teenager around him. Yet she couldn't help herself or stop her body's reaction to his presence.

"Jell-O spoons sound perfect. Let's find a movie and call it a night."

She swallowed hard, trying to sound normal when she spoke. "Sure. Sounds like a plan."

She was in so much trouble.

Tessa grabbed the bowl from the fridge as well as two spoons while Murphy got them each a glass of water. Since she wasn't about to drink around him when he couldn't, and they were about to inhale way too much sugar, water was the best option. They moved into the living room, each taking a seat on opposite sides of the couch.

They each took a spoon and dug into the dessert, barely watching the movie and not quite talking about anything important. Sugar pumped into her system, and yet she didn't feel hyper. No, she was beyond antsy and had no idea what she was doing.

"This feels weird," Murphy said after a moment since neither of them had spoken for a bit.

Tessa let out a breath and set her water down on the table in front of them. "It *is* weird." She hadn't wanted it to be weird. But she didn't know how to move on with things so tense and them both trying to be overly polite. Murphy scooted closer, and Tessa sucked in a breath. She could feel the heat of him, and a small part of her knew doing anything tonight would change everything. Yet the other part of her wanted to move even closer and feel every inch of him. There was something truly wrong with her, and yet right then, she didn't care.

"I know you told me to forget what happened after I got out of the shower, but I don't think I can." Murphy turned toward her, and she moved her head so she looked right into his eyes. She almost gasped at the heat she saw in them, and at how dark they'd become, but she stopped just in time.

"What are you saying?"

"I can't get you out of my head, Tessa." Murphy raked his hands through his hair, and Tessa watched as his muscles bunched up deliciously at the action. "We've always flirted, but we made sure to stay on the side of friendship."

"And that was a good choice," Tessa said quickly, afraid of what was being said, and yet knowing there was no turning back now.

"Was it? Because I'm so happy that you're in my life. I love that you're my friend. But every time I look at you, I see something more. I see something that we *could* be."

"Are you talking about just sex?" She wasn't sure she wanted to hear the answer, but she needed to know. "Because I'm not going to ruin what we have. I'm not going to ruin what our friends have just for sex. I might be damn good at sex and, hell, I'm pretty sure you're damn good at it, too, but no amount of sex is worth ruining everything else."

Murphy snorted. "I *am* damn good at sex. And I have a

feeling you're even better than you think you are, but that's not what I'm talking about. Or, at least, that's not *all* I'm talking about. I like you. I think I've always liked you. I don't know what's coming for me—or anyone else for that matter. But I'm tired of standing by and doing nothing because I'm too afraid of what might happen."

Tears filled her eyes, and Murphy reached out to wipe them away before she could. "Murphy…"

"I didn't mean to make you cry. I don't ever want to make you cry. I want to feel your skin beneath my fingertips. I want to know what you feel like against me when we both plan on it, and not when it's by accident. I want to know who you are beyond the woman that I know now because I have a feeling that woman is fucking amazing."

"Murphy…you're going to have to explain to me exactly what you're saying because, right now? Right now, I'm seriously confused." Or rather, she was afraid she was reading too much into his words and getting it all wrong.

Murphy moved closer again, this time, so close that their thighs touched, and she could feel his breath on her neck. "I'm saying you only live once, Tessa. I want to know you. I want to feel you underneath me. I want to go back to your bedroom and make love to you, fuck you hard into the mattress until we are both sweaty, panting, and spent. What comes after? That's something we'll have to figure out as we go on, but I'm tired of holding myself back because I'm afraid. I'm tired of not doing what could be the best thing for us because I don't want to take the chance."

He cupped her face, and she sucked in a breath. The heat of him was unreal, and all she wanted to do was lean forward and brush her lips over his. But she couldn't. Not yet. Tessa might have always been a risk taker, but what they had was far too important to risk. *Murphy* was far too important to risk.

"Are you saying all of this because you're sick?" She asked the one question she knew he might hate her for. But it was also the question she needed the answer to most.

"Maybe. But I've been feeling this need for you since before I knew I was sick again. So, maybe me looking into the hourglass made me actually give in to what I'm feeling. But knowing that isn't the reason I want you in the first place. I want you, Tessa. All of you. Not because I'm afraid of what might come, but because I don't want to lose what we could have *because* of fear."

She had no idea what to say. She had no idea what would be a good answer. She had been battling her attraction to Murphy since the beginning, and she knew he'd always been attracted to her, as well. But now, she felt as if they were both at the tipping point. So instead of talking more, instead of worrying, instead of thinking that she was possibly making a huge mistake, she just *felt*.

And damned the consequences in the morning.

Murphy's hand tightened in her hair, and she leaned forward and finally brushed her lips along his. He sucked in a breath and parted his lips. Their tongues tangled as they deepened the kiss, moaning into each other's mouths. Tessa slid her hands up Murphy's sides and over his chest to brush her fingers along his jaw. She didn't think, she'd promised she wouldn't. She just kissed him.

He tasted of sugar, sin, and Murphy. The rough stubble of his beard tickling her fingertips just turned her on even more. Somehow, he moved, and she found herself on her back with Murphy hovered over her, their mouths never leaving one another. She wrapped her legs around his waist, arching her back to press her breasts into his chest. The memory of the last time her breasts had pressed against him made her even wetter. This time, they weren't naked— yet—and they weren't impacted by surprise. *This* time, it would be actions of their choosing, and she wanted to remember every feeling, every moan, every taste.

She wanted to remember Murphy.

Murphy's fingers skimmed over her skin as he slowly stripped off her shirt. She shivered as the cool air of the house touched her skin, but before she could even process it all, his lips were on her body, licking, sucking, and kissing every inch of bare skin within reach.

He looked like a man possessed, and she knew her own face mirrored that. She *craved* him with such intensity that it scared her, so she slid her hands through his hair and pushed all thoughts of what could happen later out of her head. She would live in the moment and relish his taste and touch. He was already far better than even her wildest dreams, and they were still mostly dressed, and no one had come.

Yet.

With her help, Murphy undid her bra, and she threw it behind her, knowing she needed his lips on her nipples.

"Your tits are fucking amazing, babe." He cupped her breasts together, squeezing them ever so slightly, brushing her nipples with the pads of his thumbs. Since she'd lowered her legs so he could position himself better, she couldn't press her thighs together like she wanted to, so she pressed her legs into his thighs instead.

"You're going to make me come just like that," she breathed.

"Yeah?" Murphy asked, his eyes bright. "Have you ever come by having a man suck on your nipples without touching your clit?"

She shook her head. "Never...but...but I'm already so close just by having you on top of me."

Murphy leaned down and sucked her nipple into his mouth, keeping his eyes on hers. It was the sexiest thing she'd ever seen in her life, and she'd seen the man naked and wet. She gasped when he bit down on one breast while plucking her other nipple with his fingers. When he added his tongue, twisting and sucking, she closed her eyes, the sensation of seeing his dark head above her too much for her to handle. She'd always had sensitive nipples, and used them along with playing with her clit often when she masturbated, but all of that was nothing compared to what Murphy Gallagher did to her.

When he hummed and sent shivers straight to her clit

even though she was still wearing jeans and he hadn't even touched her there yet, she came, arching into him and moaning his name at the same time.

"Holy..." She couldn't even finish that thought because he had his mouth on hers in the next instant, taking in her words and her breaths. Somehow, she found the energy to push up his shirt, as well. She needed to see him, feel him. He moved away from her just enough so she could peel his shirt off of him and pull it over his head. When he looked down at her, she lost all sense of what she had been thinking about before and softly raked her hands down his chest, somehow finding the strength to pull back enough not to hurt him since he bruised so easily.

Her hand went to the bruise on his hip that had spread from where the showerhead had hit him, and she bit her lip, sadness creeping up and spreading through her.

Murphy lifted her chin and stared intensely into her eyes. "Don't think about that. Don't think about anything except you and me and what we're doing right now. I'm fine, I'm here. I'm here with you. So stop worrying and let me get your pants off so I can eat you out. How does that sound?"

Tessa laughed at the sudden change in his tone and planted her feet on the couch so she could lift her butt. "Jeans off. Got it." She winked even though fear for what that bruise meant was still on her mind, just as she knew it was on Murphy's. But they both needed this right now, needed each other, and she'd give him that.

He undid the button of her jeans, and she bit her lip. As

he slowly slid the denim and her panties down her legs, she met his gaze, needing him more than she ever thought possible.

"Get naked," she panted. "I want to see you."

"You just want to see my piercing."

"That is true. Your beautiful dick has nothing to do with it."

Murphy barked out a laugh and stood up so he could take off his jeans and boxer briefs. When he gripped his already hard cock, she slid her hand between her legs to brush over her clit. She was already so wet, she should have been embarrassed, but she saw the moisture on the tip of his dick and knew she wasn't alone in her need.

"Aw, baby, do you think my dick is pretty?"

"You know your dick is pretty. I bet you admire it in the mirror every morning."

"You caught me. Little Murphy is quite fetching. It's why he has jewelry now and everything."

She rolled her eyes and started to touch herself. She was already so tender and swollen from her orgasm, but she needed more. Murphy reached between her legs and dipped his finger inside her. Before she could gasp and arch into him, however, he moved his hand back to his cock and used her wetness to slick his hand up and down his cock. Soon, they were both moving their hands fast, bringing themselves closer and closer to orgasm.

"You are so fucking hot right now. Are you thinking of my cock inside you right now in place of those fingers? Am I fucking you hard? Making you want to come? Talk to me, Tessa."

She licked her lips, increasing the speed of her hand. "It's you. It's always you. Hell, I've been coming on my own thinking of you for months now."

She would have hated herself for admitting that if Murphy's eyes hadn't gone dark at that exact moment.

"I stroke off way too fucking much thinking of you. I'm going to end up with chafing burns one of these days from jacking off to you."

Tessa arched her back, fingering herself as he stroked his dick. They weren't even touching each other, and it was the single most erotic moment of her life.

"I'm coming," she panted.

"Good," Murphy growled.

They came together, her body shaking as her inner muscles squeezed her fingers. Murphy spurted over his lower belly, grunting as he squeezed his dick even harder and played with the ring on the tip.

Before she could come down from her high and let herself be disappointed that he hadn't come inside her, he'd cleaned himself off and had her legs over his shoulders in the next instant.

"What?" she asked, her body already on alert again and ready to climb that peak.

"I told you I was going to eat you out. And while I'm doing that to make you come a couple more times, I should be ready to go again so I can fuck you hard into the cushion. How does that sound?"

"That sounds like I'm going to be walking funny tomorrow," she teased. "I've never come more than three times in a night, and that was with a vibrator, not a man."

Murphy clucked his tongue before licking her in one long swipe. She shivered, clamping her thighs around his head. "I'll have to change that, won't I?" And when his stubble scraped her inner thighs, she knew this man just might wring every damn orgasm she had out of her until she was a puddle of sex and limbs.

He licked and sucked at her, using his fingers until she was ready to scream his name and tug on his hair so he'd fuck her already. But the damn man refused to budge until she orgasmed on his face. And since he looked so sexy with his dark hair between her legs, and his tongue was a master all on its own, she came not once, but *twice* on his face.

She wasn't sure she could take any more, but as soon as she saw Murphy standing and slowly rolling the condom over his cock, she knew she could at least try one more time.

Murphy knelt on one end of the couch, gripped her hips, met her gaze, and thrust into her wet heat in one demanding movement. They both cried out, her inner muscles so swollen and tender from multiple orgasms that she was afraid she might not make it, but she knew she'd never felt anything like this and wouldn't again.

This was *Murphy*.

Her Murphy.

Then he moved.

He did as promised and made love to her, at the same time fucking her until they both came hard, her body going limp while Murphy shouted her name, filling the condom. When he turned them so he could tuck her into his side with his semi-hard cock still buried deeply within her, she knew she might have made a mistake. She wouldn't regret what she'd done with Murphy, but she had a feeling she wouldn't want to let him go. Ever.

This wasn't just sex. It had never been about sex. And that was the problem.

11

Murphy stared down at Tessa's sleeping form and prayed they hadn't made a mistake. After they'd fallen on top of each other on the couch, and he'd taken care of the condom, they laid there for another few minutes before they stumbled into her bedroom and fell asleep in a pile of limbs. He'd woken her up in the middle of the night and slowly made love to her by holding her back to his front, slowly thrusting into her from behind until they both came and fell asleep again. He would be sore for the rest of the day and knew Tessa would feel it even more. But now, in the light of day, he was afraid she'd want to take it all back. He had never met another woman like Tessa, and he wanted to know her more. He wanted to see who they could be if they were together and not just Murphy and Tessa: roommates. They had been friends, then roommates, and now, he hoped they could be something more. But he had seen the fear in her eyes the night before, and had been afraid that would happen. They would have to talk, and he had no idea where to start.

Tessa mumbled in her sleep and buried herself closer to him. Murphy ran his hand through her hair, trying not to wake her. He just needed to keep touching her, as if he were afraid if he stopped, everything would go back to the way it was before last night. He could still feel her on his skin, in his *soul*, so he knew it hadn't been a dream. Yet part of him was afraid it had been.

He hadn't been lying to her when he'd said he didn't want to worry about the future. Though that didn't mean he wasn't worried about the future. Hell, all he did these days was wonder about what would happen. He was worried about Max. He was worried about himself. He was worried whether he would have a future at all. Hell, he was even worried about the fact that he had forgotten to tell Tessa that he'd met her parents. How stupid and idiotic was he that he had not mentioned to her that her parents were planning to remodel their home? With Gallagher Brothers Restoration. It had honestly slipped his mind with so much going on. Between his illness, work, Tessa, and the fact that Brent had ended his relationship with her all during the same time, it had literally slipped his mind. He didn't know how she would react to the fact that her parents wanted to work with the Gallaghers, but telling her while they were both in bed, naked, after spending their first night together making passionate love until the wee hours of the morning?

That would've probably been the most idiotic thing he could've done.

And now, here he was, somewhat keeping a secret from her while naked in her bed, and had no idea what he was going to say when she opened her eyes. Did he want a relationship with her? Dammit, of course, he did. He'd wanted one with her even before he found out he was sick. He'd hit on her in that bar, and had wanted her from that first moment. But he'd been so afraid of what would happen if it didn't work out that he hadn't taken that step. That was just careless. Being afraid of what *could* happen if things didn't work out meant not taking the risk at all. By not taking the risk, you could lose out on something greater than any disappointment in the end.

And from what he knew of Tessa, she could be something far more than a fling. For a man who had spent so long trying not to think of the exact type of person he could settle down with, he was surprised at the idea that it could be Tessa. Yes, it was moving way too fast, but it wasn't like he didn't know her. Of course, he didn't know everything about her, and he didn't know if he loved her. But the idea that he *could* love her told him that he needed to step carefully and not mess this up before it had even started. Murphy had spent the beginning of his life trying not to think about death and yet staring it in the face every day with every breath. And when he'd gotten healthy and finally walked through that veil of uncertainty, he hadn't wanted to think about who he could be with or what he could become if he were to fall for someone. He had wanted to find out the man he could be without that end in sight. He had gone into business with his brothers, but had always been a step apart. He had rented a home instead of buying one. The first thing he'd ever bought was his truck, and that was for work, considering he carried around heavy materials all day from site to site. It wasn't as if he never thought to settle down; he just hadn't pictured whom that could possibly be with. And now that he was thinking it could potentially be the woman in his arms, he was surprisingly calm.

Okay, maybe *calm* wasn't the right word. He was still anxious about the fact that he had no idea what Tessa would say when she woke up. And he knew he was moving far too fast in some respects since he wasn't even sure they were *together*, but he wanted to find out more about her. For that to happen, however, he had to make sure she didn't run away at the first sign of tension.

In other words, Murphy had no idea what he was doing.

At that moment, Tessa blinked awake, and Murphy did his best not to tense up.

"Good morning." He traced her jaw with his finger, loving the soft skin underneath his touch.

She didn't tense up, but neither did she lean into his caress. She looked just as confused as he felt, and he knew they would have to talk. He just didn't know what he needed to say.

"Hi," she said softly.

"Uh..."

She smiled slightly and let out a breath. "We should get up or we'll be late to work."

He leaned down and kissed her lips. "We should talk, though."

She looked up into his eyes, confusion on her face, but when she nodded, a small knot in his belly relaxed—marginally. "I know. But...after work. I...I don't want to say something I don't mean because I'm not awake or confused. Okay?"

He let out a breath, understanding and agreeing with her even if he was a little disappointed. He had never reacted this way to another woman before, and it confused him. "After work, then?"

She winced. "I promised Liz I'd go wedding dress shopping after work."

"Shit. I promised my brothers I'd hang out with them tonight anyway since Owen wanted to talk a few things out. I had forgotten. Tomorrow?"

She shook her head. "I have dinner at my parents' tomorrow."

Murphy stiffened and opened his mouth to tell her about her parents' visit, then froze as her alarm went off.

She let out a short laugh and sat up, pulling her sheet up to cover her breasts. "I need to get ready or I'll be late, and my boss gets pissy if I'm even just on time. But, Murph? I don't regret anything. I don't do regrets. At least, I try not to. But I need time to think about what it all means. So, after

I do dinner at my parents', let's sit and talk about everything."

He sat up with her and brought her close for a kiss. God, he could get addicted to her taste. "I'm glad you don't have regrets. Because I don't either. I just..."

His phone went off in the living room, and she laughed. "That's your alarm, Murph. Let's get going for the day and then we'll figure out what the hell we're doing." She stood up, gave him a quick kiss, and fled to the bathroom.

Well, that could have been worse, even though it hadn't been the reaction he'd hoped for. Instead of staring after her like some lovesick fool, he went into the living room and turned off the alarm on his phone. Then he picked up his clothes, the condom wrapper, and everything else they had left out the night before, and went back to his bedroom so he could finish getting ready for the day. He had installed a temporary showerhead in the guest bathroom so he would be able to use that one instead of her shower that morning. However, he knew he would have to change it out later for one that she would actually like in her house. It felt weird, picking things out for a house that wasn't his, and yet one he lived in. It was part of his job to help pick out the little things like showerheads when restoring a building, and yet doing so for Tessa felt like something different.

And...he was officially losing it if he was sitting here thinking about the intricacies of bathroom fixtures and how they connected to a relationship.

Like he'd said before, he was in so much trouble.

. . .

BY THE TIME he got out of the shower and dressed for the day, Tessa was already gone. She must have gotten ready at the speed of light so she could run out before she had to see him again. He hoped it was just nerves and not anything worse. Yet there was still doubt. He made his way to the main Gallagher offices to meet up with his brothers. They still had two small, ongoing projects, but their crew would be working without them that morning. He and his brothers had a few things that would be easier to go through at the main offices rather than at the small trailer they kept at some of the sites. Even Jake would be there, even though the man didn't always attend these meetings. But since Murphy knew they would be talking about the large, potential, upcoming project—a.k.a. Tessa's family's remodel—all of the Gallaghers would be there.

And once again, Murphy was reminded that he was an idiot for not mentioning it to Tessa at first. Hopefully, she wouldn't be too angry since nothing was set in stone. He wouldn't sign a single piece of paper or meet with her parents again until he spoke with Tessa. He already had enough riding on his relationship with her as it was. He wasn't going to add stupid secrets and misunderstandings to the mix.

As soon as he walked into the office, he knew he'd made a mistake. He might've washed Tessa's scent from his skin, and he might've showered and tried to look completely normal, but there was no way his brothers weren't going to figure out that something was different with him.

"You slept with Tessa," Jake said the moment Murphy walked into the room.

"What?" Murphy set down his briefcase and tried not to look his brother in the eye. It was no use.

"I know that look, I've *had* that look." Graham shook his head. "That's the well-lubed-by-a-woman-you-actually-like look. I'm pretty sure I had that look for the first month I was with Blake. Hell, I'm sure I *still* have that look most mornings."

Owen narrowed his eyes. "You're going to fuck this up, Murph. You're going to fuck this up, and someone is going to get hurt. And if my pregnant, soon-to-be wife gets upset because you've fucked this up and hurt her friend in the process, I'm going to get pissed off."

Angry and confused, Murphy looked at his brother and then turned to the other two in the room as he shook his head. "Why on earth do you think I'm the one who's going to ruin everything? I have spent months being her friend. Hell, I *am* her friend. She's quickly becoming one of my best friends. She opened her home to me."

"And you thought it would be a good idea to sleep with her?" Owen scowled.

"I think I'm falling in love with her," Murphy blurted and then rubbed his eyes. "Fuck. Forget I said that. I don't even know if that's true. But I really like her, and I never would have done anything to jeopardize what she and I have together. I know it's complicated because we're all connected, but damn, man, I'm not going to sit back and let her walk away because I'm afraid. I'm not going to be afraid anymore. I spent most of my life scared of one thing or another and never having the power to do anything about it. But what's going on between Tessa and me, that's between us. Yes, everyone is going to have an opinion, and yes, everyone is going to want to tell us. But no matter what, in the end, it's between her and me. I don't know what's going to happen, but I want to find out. Do you really think I would've taken this step without thinking about what could happen? Of course, I thought about what could happen. I've spent *months* thinking about what could happen. But she is worth it, guys. Tessa is worth it."

Jake blew out a breath. "I never heard you sound so passionate before, man. If she gets you this riled up after just one night with her, I can't wait to see what happens next."

"You know we'll always worry about you." Graham started to take a step forward but seemed to think better of it. "I think Tessa could be great for you, but she has a lot of baggage. Maybe more than you, which is saying something, considering us Gallaghers have enough baggage to fill a couple of airplanes. But I like the way she makes you smile. I always have. It's why I tease you so relentlessly. And while we're worried about what could happen, it's because we don't want anything to hurt you. You're already going through so much, but if Tessa can make that better, then I'll stand right by your side and do what I can to help."

Surprised at how Graham was reacting, Murphy looked over to Owen and hoped his brother could understand. "And what about you, Owen? Do you have anything else to say, or do you think I'm just going to screw it all up like I screw up everything?"

"I think I hope you guys know what you're doing. But I also know that you're my baby brother, and I would do anything for you. I've always wanted you to be happy. Always." Owen cleared his throat before bending over his desk and riffling through a few pieces of paper. "We have a few things to go over today before we head out to the sites. I know Tessa's parents want to meet with us this week to go over what they want done to see if we can actually give them that." Owen looked up and gave Murphy a look. "You going to be okay with us working with her folks?"

Murphy blew out a breath. "It should be fine. Except I need to talk to Tessa about it first." He held his hands out, quelling his brothers' questioning looks. "I know, I know. I need to talk to her, but we've been a little busy with other things."

Each brother gave him a knowing look this time, and Murphy flipped them off. "That's not exactly what I meant. But I do need to talk to Tessa before you make any other decisions. I know it's risky mixing business with pleasure, but come on, our whole family is mixing business with pleasure at this point."

Graham nodded, a wide smile on his face. "Yeah, that's pretty much our new motto now. Just make sure you talk to Tessa quickly before this becomes an actual issue. I do think we could work wonders on that home if we get the job. It would be something interesting for all of us, and the project has little pieces that are prime for each of our wheelhouses."

"I agree." Owen nodded and tapped a few things into his ever-present tablet. "So, let's see how this week goes. We'll finish up the other projects we have slated for the week and then get through everything else."

The four of them talked some more about where each of them would be going for the day before breaking off to actually do more hands-on work. While Murphy was technically the lead architect for the company, they weren't that big-time yet that he was allowed to just sit back and not do any hands-on work. He didn't have as much energy as he used to thanks to the fact that, yes, he did have cancer, but he could at least do some things. His team and his brothers didn't let him overwork himself. And because he wanted to get healthy and beat this sickness, he wasn't going to let himself overdo it.

Things are changing, Murphy thought. He just had to make sure he could find a way to keep up.

12

Tessa packed up her things and glanced at the clock. If she wasn't quick, she might end up being late to her family dinner, and she had promised herself she wouldn't be late to one of them again. It wasn't that she tried to not make it on time; it was just that everything kept getting in the way. Even if she were late, her parents wouldn't mind, they would just smile and say they were happy to see her. But she would still feel bad for not showing up when she should.

She loved her parents so much, and she knew they loved her just as much as they would love any biological children they had. It had taken too long for her to realize that fact, and she had acted out because of it. She hadn't liked the Tessa she was before she became the woman she was now. If she could have gone back to meet her teenage self, she probably would've slapped the kid upside the head and told her to get over herself. But since she couldn't do that, she ended up hating herself just a little bit more every time she saw her parents. And, really, it had nothing to do with them. It was all her own guilt.

And that was enough of that line of thinking for the moment. No wonder she hadn't slept the night before. She and Liz had gotten home late, and Murphy had already been in bed since he'd been tired from lack of sleep the night before and treatments. He'd left her a note on her pillow that she may or may not have hidden in her nightstand so she could look at it later.

So, now, she hadn't been able to truly speak with Murphy. And that morning, she had practically run from him and into the bathroom so she could get ready for the day after they'd made love all night. Having sex with Murphy may have been the best experience of her life, yet she still hadn't been able to process it all. Work was slowly sucking the life out of her and making her head hurt more and more every day, and she was trying to juggle that, this upcoming dinner with her parents, Liz, and now Murphy. Not to mention the fact that she'd recently gotten dumped by Brent and had just seen her ex in Denver.

It was all a little much, and she needed a day off to just breathe and think things through. Unfortunately, she didn't see an end in sight, and she still had to go figure out what to say to Murphy when they actually got time to sit down and talk about what had happened.

Not that she'd been avoiding him.

Much.

She waved at others as she passed them, heading out for the day, and walked to her car. As soon as she sat down, she frowned. Something felt...off. She couldn't quite explain it, but it was as if a few things had been moved around. Not much, but things like her phone charger were at different angles than what she remembered.

"That's weird..." She looked around the parking lot but didn't see anyone. And, honestly, she couldn't think *why* things felt so weird. Maybe she was just a little too tired and losing it. After all, she'd been in a fog that morning just like the previous morning when she'd fled from Murphy into her bedroom. She'd probably just moved things around and hadn't noticed.

Putting away those thoughts for later, she started on her way to her parents' house. They only lived twenty minutes away from the hospital if she caught the green lights and didn't take the highway during rush hour. That was one of the many things she loved about Denver. Most suburbs were pretty easy to get to as long as you stayed off the major roads.

Her phone rang through her Bluetooth on her way to her parents'. She answered, not knowing whom it could be since her phone hadn't paired fully and she didn't recognize the number.

"Hello?"

"Tessa? Hey, it's Murphy. I just wanted to call and make sure you're okay." He paused, and Tessa bit her lip. She didn't want to think about the fact that she really loved hearing his voice. "I mean, I'm sure you're okay. I just haven't really seen you for a bit. You're on your way to your parents', right?"

Tessa nodded and changed lanes before remembering that he couldn't actually see her. "I'm on my way there now, but I'm running late since work wouldn't let me leave when I wanted to. But that's what happens sometimes." She turned onto her parents road, still unsure how tonight would go since it had been a couple of weeks since she'd seen her mom and dad and was still confused regarding what to do with Murphy. Tessa was never one to not know what she was doing or why she was doing it. But she'd never felt as lost as she did right then. But with Murphy, all rules and prior actions seemed to go out the window. "When I get back tonight after dinner, we can talk." She winced at how that sounded, yet she wasn't sure what else to say. She was attracted to Murphy, yes, and she really liked him. But she wasn't sure what he wanted, nor was she sure that being with him was the best thing for either of them. And, sometimes, honestly, she just thought too much.

"Yeah, I'll be waiting for you when you get home." It was weird hearing him talk about her house as his home, and yet it wasn't as weird as it should have been. That might've been a warning sign; one that Tessa would just have to ignore for now. "I did call for a reason, though. I have to tell you something, do you have a few seconds?"

Tessa frowned at the uncertainty in his voice but

couldn't comment on it because she had just pulled into her parents' driveway. Her mother immediately walked out onto the porch as if she had been waiting for Tessa all along. Knowing her mom, that was probably the case. Tessa didn't spend as much time with them she wanted to, and it was her fault. She just always felt so awkward and didn't know how to act in certain situations.

"I actually just pulled in. My mom's waiting for me on the porch, so why don't you just tell me when I get home later tonight. Got to go. Thanks for calling, Murph." She paused. "It's good to hear your voice."

Murphy was silent for a few seconds, and she was afraid she'd said the wrong thing. "Yeah, it's good to hear your voice, too. I can't wait to see you. All of you." There was a growl to his voice that sent shivers over Tessa's spine as she blushed.

She hung up and turned off the car before getting out to greet her mom. While Tessa was all curves and some height, her adoptive parents were long and lean, with pale skin and really blond hair. Some people would've killed for that kind of dye job, and yet it came naturally to the two people who had raised her. There were a few strands of white starting to show in both of their hair now, but Tessa thought it just made them look more stunning. Tessa's hair was dark, and her skin tanned a little easier than her folks'. She knew she really didn't look anything like them. It had bothered her when she was a child because she had felt out of place when everyone had constantly commented that she didn't

look like her parents. People were so inconsiderate about
the fact that yes, she'd been adopted, But her parents had
loved her with every ounce of their being. They still did.
Now she didn't mind the fact that she didn't look like them.
There were just too many things on her mind for her to
worry about something as silly as that. If only she could find
a way to make sure the people who had loved her uncondi-
tionally understood that she appreciated them more than
she could ever say. Yet, she had no idea where to begin. And
because of that, she would just continue to feel as awkward
as ever and a little out of place. And that was on her.

"Tessa! I'm so glad you're here." Grace Stone opened her
arms wide, and Tessa moved in to hug her mom. She didn't
remember calling Grace anything but "Mom," but she'd
been young when she was adopted. Sometimes, there were
flashes of memory or dreams where she'd think of Grace as
Grace and not her mom, but she wasn't sure those were
even real. She was afraid it had always been her subconscious trying to actively ruin the best thing that had ever
happened to her.

The Stones had been the best parents in the world to
her, and Tessa had acted out because she'd felt as if she
weren't good enough. That had all been on her, though.
Grace and Chris had never once made her feel unloved or
unwanted. Yet, somehow, Tessa had twisted that into something else. As if she had been trying to force them into
proving their love when she was a teenager. It had been
horrid and cowardly, and Tessa had never been more

ashamed. She'd ended up in the back of a police car more than once because of it, and she could only blame herself.

And while she knew they never blamed her, she'd never been able to find her way back to *not* feeling like she'd disappointed them. It might be in been in her head, but she had no idea how to fix it.

"I'm glad I'm here too, Mom." Tessa held Grace close and sighed, closing her eyes to inhale that sugar and floral scent that told her that her mom had been baking after she'd put on her perfume that morning.

"Let's get you inside. Your dad is firing up the grill because we're having kebobs. I've been letting them marinate for a couple hours now."

Tessa's stomach growled, and she laughed as Grace patted her tummy like she had when she was a little girl. "I think I've become so spoiled by your food that it's hard for me to want to cook at home."

"I like spoiling you, baby. It makes me feel like I'm doing something right." Her mom led her through the entryway and the foyer, then past the family room and the living room and into the large kitchen. Much of the house had remained the same from when Tessa was a little girl. They had remodeled some of it but not everything over the years. The place was a three-story mini mansion with lots of history, just not as much as others in the US. Considering they were in Colorado and the homes just weren't as old as those out east. Her family had money, that was for sure, but they were also pretty frugal about what they spent their hard-earned dollars on. Tessa credited them with teaching her how to save her pennies even if she had more than nickels and dimes in the bank. And though she hadn't let them help her buy her first home, their lessons in how to spend and save money had helped her save her down payment in the first place.

It had always been a little weird to her how much money her parents actually had. She'd gone from living in a rat hole apartment with a drugged out mom and an absent father, straight to living with possibly the best foster, soon-to-be adoptive parents in the world. When she had been younger, she couldn't quite handle that. She'd ended up living up to her birth parents' expectations by having sex *far* too young, drinking when she shouldn't, and taking up smoking even though she never got the inhaling part down. She'd tried to be the bad girl when she truly had no reason to be.

She'd been an idiot teenager who hurt the two people that cared for her the most. And because of that, she was still a little distant. Tessa wanted to change that and was slowly working her way up to it, but it wasn't easy when she had no idea what she was doing.

"Tessa-bean, you're here." Chris Stone, her father and all around great man beamed at her from the grill on the back deck. Tessa squeezed her mother's hand before going over to her father and giving him a hug. He hugged her back with both arms, squeezing her tightly. Her dad gave some of the best hugs, and before she'd met the

Gallaghers, she'd assumed they were the best in the world.

The Gallaghers gave great hugs, too.

"Something smells amazing," Tessa said, her stomach growling once again.

"Your mom is the best cook I know," her dad said with a wink. "I just stand over the grill and pretend I know what I'm doing while she directs me. I'm one lucky man."

Tessa grinned, feeling more relaxed than she'd been in a while. "That you are."

"Anything new going on?" her mom asked as she handed over an iced tea with fresh lemon on the rim of the glass. "How is Brent?"

Tessa winced. She'd told her parents about Brent in passing, shortly before he'd dumped her. Since she hadn't dated anyone seriously since her disaster of a relationship with her ex, she was careful about whom she mentioned. "We aren't going out anymore, sadly."

Her dad shook his head. "Do you want me to beat him up for you? Now that you aren't a minor, it makes it a little easier for me to do things like that, you know."

Tessa laughed. "Thanks for the offer. Murphy actually already said he'd beat him up for me. And I'm sure the other Gallaghers would join in."

Her mom smiled wide. "Of course, they would. They're good boys. Liz talks about Owen all the time when I get her on the phone, you know. That's why we're using them."

Tessa frowned. "Huh? Using who."

"Grace," her dad chided gently. "I thought that was going to be a surprise for after dinner."

Her mom waved him off. "Oh, drat. I can never keep a secret." She clasped her hands together in front of her and bounced like a schoolgirl, her eyes dancing. "We're remodeling the house, Tessa-bean, and having the Gallaghers do it. We haven't signed the paperwork yet, but it's as good as done. We figured it was time to update a few things structurally that would help us as we get older, but also just make the place a little more open. Then we get to decorate, as well; though the Gallaghers said they can help there, too."

Tessa blinked, shock running through her body. "You've met with them?" She tried to act casual, but she was anything but. *No one* had mentioned this to her. Not Liz, or hell, not Murphy. She lived with the man, had *slept* with him, and he hadn't commented on the fact that he'd met with her parents about updating her childhood home.

"We have, though we were waiting to talk to you tonight about it and surprise you before we went through with it all," Grace said with a grin. "Surprise! We're working with Liz's new family! And now that you're living with Murphy, it's like we're all one big, happy family."

Tessa smiled and hoped it reached her eyes. Everyone had kept her in the dark, and she wasn't sure how she felt about that. Hell, she wasn't sure how she felt about the fact that Murphy would be working with her parents at all. Not only didn't she like secrets, but it was also weird to her how her worlds kept colliding. *It shouldn't matter*, she told herself. And yet, somehow, it did. And Murphy hadn't told her.

Murphy Gallagher was in for it when she got home, that much she knew.

13

"He's sleeping right now, I'm sorry," Abby said into the phone, her voice hushed. "He's almost done with treatment, but he's been so tired lately. I'll let him know you called, though." Max's fiancée sounded worried, and Murphy did his best to reassure her. Abby would know more about Max's health than he would, but he still didn't like knowing that his friend's girl was upset.

"No worries," Murphy said, keeping his tone light. "I was just going to see if he wanted to catch a game or something at the pub near me."

"Oh, I'm sure he'd love that, just not tonight, you know?"

"Give him my best," Murphy said. "And take care of yourself, as well, okay?"

"I am. Max doesn't let me overdo it. He's a good man like that.

"The best," Murphy agreed before ending the call. While he waited for Tessa to get home, Murphy had thought to hang out with Max out of the treatment center since he didn't have any other plans. His brothers were off doing things with their significant others, and Murphy didn't want to spend the evening at home making himself worry and stress. He wasn't into the bar scene anymore, but his local pub had decent food and always had the best games on TV no matter the sport. He figured he'd eat his way through nachos and chicken wings and wait for Tessa to come home. He'd spent the earlier part of the day feeling like crap and throwing up everything he'd had to eat the night before. But his appetite was back, and he didn't want to think about what he should be eating instead of junk food. Some days, cancers sucked all the life out of him, and all he wanted to do was forget about that fact that his body was trying to kill him and act normally. That wasn't easy most days.

His phone buzzed, and he looked down at the screen, surprised when he looked at the contact name. "Hey, Hugh, nice to hear from you," he answered. He hadn't thought his childhood friend would call him again after their awkward meeting before. It hadn't honestly bugged him that much at the time since he hadn't gone into the meeting with any expectations. Just because they had been friends when they were in middle school and when they were teens didn't mean they would fit together now. But since Hugh was calling,

Murphy couldn't help but wonder if something had changed.

"Murphy, I just wanted to apologize for how distracted I was when I saw you downtown a few days ago. I had a few things on my mind and a couple things that came out of the blue that I wasn't prepared for. Because of that, my mind was on other matters and not on being attentive. I came off as an asshole. I'm sorry about that. So, if you were serious about wanting to catch up, I would love to grab a bite to eat with you sometime. It has been a while, and I know we have both changed since we were in our teens. But I'd love to see what you've been up to since I hear you're making a name for yourself in your family business."

Murphy smiled. "You know, I was just thinking about driving to a place nearby and getting some bar food and watching a game. I don't know if that's something you'd want to do or if you can tonight, but what do you say?"

"As it happens, I'm free tonight, so just tell me where and when and I'm game."

Murphy told Hugh where the place was and said that he'd meet him in an hour. Since he didn't want to sit at home, worrying about the fact that Tessa would probably be pissed at him when she got back, and he didn't know where they stood in terms of the relationship, he might as well see what was happening with his old friend.

If he kept busy enough, then he wouldn't think about the worries constantly plaguing his mind—and not all of them about Tessa.

Cancer.

He had fucking *cancer*.

And because this time it was a different series of treatments than the last time and he was treated as an outpatient, sometimes, it didn't feel real. He worked, he played, and he was slowly falling for his roommate, but he still had cells in his body that shouldn't be there. Without the chemo he took and the blood transfusions to keep him going, he could die.

There was no doubt about that, and yet he couldn't focus on that. He knew he was compartmentalizing to a point where he might break if he weren't careful, but if he constantly focused on things out of his control, he'd end up in a downward spiral and never heal.

Murphy slid a hand through his hair and pushed those thoughts to the corner of his mind once again. They were always there—never quiet but not quite screaming every hour of every day—but for now, he would do what he could. He'd live.

Hugh was waiting for him at one of the high-top tables near a large TV when Murphy got there. Rather than wearing slacks and a pressed shirt like he had been before, the other man wore khakis with a lighter button-down shirt that wasn't tucked in. Just casual enough to fit in with the bar scene. Murphy wore jeans but a similar button-up shirt not tucked in, so this time, he didn't feel as underdressed.

Hugh tilted his head toward him when he saw Murphy, and Murphy made his way to the table. "Glad you could make it out, man. I don't come here often, but it has a decent setup."

"Thanks for inviting me. I haven't had bar food in ages, and I'm kind of craving wings now." Hugh grinned, and Murphy saw a bit of the boy he used to know."

"Well, we came to the right place then." The two of them chatted as their waitress came over and they each ordered a couple of iced teas. Murphy wasn't sure why the other man hadn't ordered a beer, but he didn't ask. Murphy himself still couldn't drink for another couple of weeks, and frankly, he didn't like to drink even one beer these days and drive. By the time the two of them had devoured a whole plate of nachos and more than their fair share of wings, Murphy was full, a little tired, and enjoying his time with his old friend. The two of them had talked about the past and reminisced about old memories rather than talking about who they were now, but Murphy didn't mind, he was just having a good night.

"So, you said you weren't married, right?" Hugh's question seemed to come out of nowhere, but since they'd pretty much exhausted all of their other subjects, Murphy went with it.

"I'm not," Murphy frowned. "I'm sort of seeing someone. Maybe."

Hugh shook his head. "You have to be careful with women, man. These days, they want to try and take control of the relationship, and you just can't let that happen. They make things so confusing and take over. So you need to be clear on what you want and take that control back."

Murphy snorted. "Yeah, I don't really think that's the problem here."

"Well, considering you're already living with Tessa, things are bound to get complicated with any woman you date."

Murphy tilted his head and stared at the other man. "When did I mention I was rooming with Tessa?"

Hugh waved him off. "When we were talking about owning a house or something a few minutes ago. But, anyway, you should just be careful with women, man. You never know. They say they want one thing and then they go around yelling at you for another."

Maybe he had mentioned he was living with Tessa. They'd been talking about a lot of things, and most of the time, he didn't even realize when he was talking about her these days—she was always at the forefront of his mind.

"Actually, the woman I'm talking about *is* Tessa."

Hugh's eyes narrowed. "You slept with Tessa?"

"Uh, that wasn't what I was talking about, but yes, we have. And I hope we're going to be something more seri-ous." Murphy was about to say something more, but his phone buzzed at that moment, and he looked down to see Tessa's image on the screen. It was a photo he'd taken of her a few months ago when they were in Owen's back yard. She had been hanging upside down from a tree, trying to make Rowan laugh as her hair flowed around her. She'd been laughing so hard, she'd almost fallen, and Murphy had snapped a pic, loving how happy she looked. "Hold on a sec? It's her."

Hugh's jaw tightened, but he gave a small nod. "No problem."

Murphy answered, ignoring Hugh since he had Tessa on the brain. "Hey, you."

"Get your ass home right now, Murphy Gallagher." She clipped out the words. She hadn't exactly yelled, but she didn't sound happy.

He winced. Yep, she knew about the remodel. At least, he hoped that was why she was angry with him. He hadn't done anything else that he was aware of. "I'll be home soon."

"Sooner than soon, Gallagher."

"Leaving right now." She hung up on him, and he closed his eyes, pinching the bridge of his nose. "I got to go," he said to the other man at the table.

"Trouble with the roomie?" Hugh asked, the tension from before no longer in his face.

"Yeah, I forgot to mention something. Anyway, thanks for hanging out with me tonight. We should do this again sometime." Murphy wasn't sure if Hugh was someone he wanted to spend all his time with, but it was nice getting to know the man again. Murphy didn't have a lot of friends outside of his family as it was thanks to his busy schedule.

"Sounds good. Be careful," Hugh warned. "Women can be mean."

Murphy shrugged. "I kind of deserve it." They said their goodbyes, and Murphy headed home, hoping Tessa would be slightly calmer by the time he got there. What he'd done wasn't *too* bad, and it hadn't exactly been his fault, but still.

He wanted this to work with Tessa. What *this* was? That was something they would have to talk about, but he wanted her to be part of his life, and he knew she felt the same way, even if he didn't know exactly what part of her life she wanted him to be in.

When he walked into the house, Tessa stood in the living room, her arms folded over her chest and a frown on her face.

"Why didn't you tell me?"

"Your parents told you, then?" he asked, closing the door behind him.

She raised her brow. "Is there something else you haven't told me?"

He shook his head and took a step toward her. She didn't back away—progress—but she didn't look receptive to him getting any closer either. "I didn't mean to keep it from you. I tried to tell you a few times, and we got distracted, or it honestly slipped my mind. I have a few other things going on right now, and sometimes, I don't remember everything." He wasn't trying to use pity to make her forgive him. He was just being honest. His brain was going in a million different directions all the time, and he was *tired*.

Her face fell, and she cupped his cheeks. He moved into

the soft touch, aching for her. "I'm sorry. I just hate being blindsided like that. My ex..." She sighed. "My ex was really good at that."

This wasn't the time to ask about the man in her past, but he would soon. He wanted to know everything about her and wanted her to know the same of him.

"I know...I'm sorry I screwed up."

"No, I get it. I just...gah. Can you just kiss me and let's forget everything else for the night?"

His heart raced, and he took a step closer so they were chest-to-chest. "I can do that, babe, but if I do that, I'm not going to stop kissing you. And in the morning, I'm going to want to drink coffee with you. I'm going to want to know about you, *be* with you. I'll want real dates and smiling and holding each other in public. I'm greedy. I want it all." He hadn't meant to blurt all of that out, but he'd needed to say it.

Her eyes widened, and her mouth parted. "I...I'm not really good at being a girlfriend."

Girlfriend. Hell, he loved that word when it pertained to her.

"I'm not good at being a boyfriend. So let's figure it out together, okay?"

"And it won't be too much?" she asked, her voice oh so quiet. "With your treatments and your job? And the fact that we live together? It all just seems like a lot."

He kissed her softly, resting his forehead on hers. "It *is* a lot, but I think we can make it work. Slowly. Just the two of us. I don't want to lose you from my life, Tessa, but I also don't want to go back to the way things were. I think that everything we were doing before led up to this moment, don't you? I've been waiting for you," he breathed. "And I didn't even know it."

"Kiss me," she repeated.

So he did.

She tasted of sweetness and all things Tessa. He craved this woman, and he didn't know how things had changed so fast. All he knew was that he had to be inside her. *Now.*

He stripped her out of her clothes so quickly, he was pretty sure he almost choked her with her bra. Considering that his dick would have permanent zipper marks from how hard he was, they made quite a pair.

"I need to taste you," he growled, going to his knees right there in the living room.

"Murphy!" Her hand tightened in his hair as he slid his tongue between her folds. He lapped at her, sucking her clit between his lips before going back to tease her with his tongue. His fingers dug into her thighs, holding her still so he could eat her out and have her come on his face.

He *loved* going down on women. There was nothing better in his world than pussy, and having his mouth on that pussy just made him thirst for more. He took his time when eating a woman out, loving each and every moment of it, and since this was *his* Tessa, he was even more attentive.

"I'm going to come," she gasped above him. Somehow,

they'd ended up by the kitchen table since they had shuffled around some. He looked up to see her leaning on the surface, her hands clamped around the edges, and her knuckles white.

"Then come," he said before sucking on her clit again. She bucked against his face, and he flicked his tongue against her, wanting her orgasm to last when she finally came. As soon as she calmed down, Murphy stood on shaky legs and stripped off his clothes after taking a condom out of his jeans. "I put a condom in my back pocket just in case, though I think we need boxes hidden around the house."

Tessa gave him a look from under hooded eyes and slowly rubbed circles around her clit with her fingers. "Sounds like a plan. Now, fuck me already."

How the hell had he gotten this lucky?

"Turn around and bend over. Press your tits to the top of the table and stick that ass up."

She raised a brow but did as he said before looking over her shoulder and wiggling that very bitable butt of hers. "Gonna fuck me in the ass?"

He gripped the base of his cock and groaned before sliding the condom over his length. With how sexy she looked, he was surprised he hadn't come right then and there just from the look of her bent over and ready for him.

"Is that something you want?" He went to her and cupped her ass, giving it a gentle squeeze. She pressed back into him, and he groaned.

"Not today since I'm not prepped, but one day soon? Totally."

He licked his lips and slid his thumb tween her folds. "Yeah? Want my dick in your ass, baby?"

She rolled her eyes even as she moaned. "I swear, mention my ass once, and suddenly, you're all growly and alpha."

Murphy grinned and used her wetness over his thumb to press against her hole. When she stiffened before pressing back against his touch, he rubbed his thumb against her.

"A little play, Tessa mine, just for now, and I'm going to fuck you hard when you're pressed on top of the table, but I need you to fuck me back. Think you can press back into me and keep up?"

In answer, she reached behind her and gripped his cock, guiding him between her legs. "Fill me up already, Gallagher. I'll go find Mr. Dildo if I need to."

He smacked her ass once, and as she arched her back into him, he filled her. Soon, they were both pumping against one another, her back arching as she met him thrust for thrust. He had one hand on her hip, keeping her steady so he didn't go too hard, too fast. The other hand was on her ass with his thumb teasing in and out of her hole.

She felt so fucking good that it was over far too soon. She came again, squeezing his dick like a vice, and he came hard, filling the condom to the brim. Their breaths came in pants, and he was having trouble seeing straight with how good she felt around him. Yet he knew this was only the beginning.

He'd never had this much fun, this much *everything* with a woman before.

Tessa Stone was something else, and Murphy couldn't wait to figure out exactly what that meant.

14

"Like the size of my club?" Murphy asked, wiggling his brows.

Tessa pinched the bridge of her nose, and he knew she was trying to keep from laughing. Nothing good could come from encouraging him in public—as she would say. Of course, he caught the twitch of her lips and just grinned wider.

She leaned forward and bit his jaw, sending shivers down his spine. And since they were indeed in public—a miniature golf course of all places—he didn't wrap his arms around her and kiss her hard. He'd just have to tally that up for later when they were alone.

"You're going to get us kicked out of miniature golf, and we will never live that down. You know that." She rolled her eyes much like Rowan was prone to do, and he just shook his head, still smiling while holding the small, bright blue golf club he'd be using while they did their nine holes. Neither of them had been sure they could do a full eighteen, even if it mostly consisted of windmills and the dreaded clown statue at hole seventeen.

No one needed to see clowns swallow your balls.

No one.

Tessa nudged his side, bringing him out of his weird thoughts. "What on earth are you thinking about? Your face just got all weird."

He leaned down and pressed a kiss to the tip of her nose. "Thanks for commenting on my looks. Good to know you're not here for just my body."

"You're an idiot. It's a wonder we've been friends this long and I haven't beaten you."

"I'd joke about that but I'm pretty sure you could take me."

"Of course, I can. But really, what were you thinking about that made your face all squinty?"

"Clowns and balls." He shuddered. "You don't want to know."

Tessa winced. "Hole seventeen? Like, what the heck were they thinking when they made that statue? It's what nightmares are made of. Oh, and ha ha on the whole ball thing. I think you're the first person ever to make a ball joke when it comes to miniature golf." Her tone was so dry he would have missed her laughter if he hadn't been looking into her eyes.

He always looked into her eyes these days, he couldn't help it.

"I love that you just *knew* why my mind went there. Well, I love it, and I'm also a little scared."

She snorted and took his hand as they started their way to the first hole. "You're one of my closest friends, and I've seen you naked, I'm pretty sure that puts us on a level where we can be dorks together. Plus, my mind is a very dirty place." She whispered that last part, though there wasn't anyone around them. It was a weeknight, and there was also a carnival opening that evening just a block away so the miniature golf place was pretty deserted. It gave Murphy more of a chance to *accidentally* brush against Tessa's very fine ass as he set up for his shot. He couldn't help it, he loved that butt. Hell, he loved every curve of her, and Little Murphy was already standing at attention, raring to go—and they hadn't even done much to get him that hard.

Murphy was going to end up with a limp by the end of the night if he weren't careful. He cleared his throat when Tessa gave him a knowing look and scanned his body. Yeah, she knew *exactly* what she did to him. But considering he'd watched her press her thighs together after they'd left the diner where he'd been whispering dirty things into her ear all night during dinner, he knew the feeling was mutual.

Not a bad way to spend the evening with your best girl.

"Ready to start?" Tessa asked. "I mean, if it takes you a few times to get it in the hole, I understand." She fluttered her eyelashes. "It's not like this would be a new thing, right?"

He snarled a bit and set up his shot again, swinging with careful accuracy and long-practiced, held-back strength.

The damn ball hit the mound in front of him and rolled right back to where it had started.

He looked up at Tessa, daring her to say anything, but she just broke out into rolling laughter, tears falling down her cheeks.

"Not one word, Tessa Stone. You make fun of my ball or how I couldn't get it into the hole on the first try, and I'll spank that ass red." He wouldn't, but since they were alone, he might as well joke with her.

She raised a brow and licked her lips. "Promise?"

Murphy let out a groan and adjusted himself, figuring he'd end up with zipper marks over his dick soon if he weren't careful. He might not have the same energy he'd had before he got sick, but Tessa gave him a boost every time he looked at her.

He wasn't sure what he thought about the full meaning of that, so he set it aside for later. *Live in the now*, he reminded himself. Just *be*.

It's all he could do.

Soft hands cupped his face, and he blinked. "Where did you go?" she whispered. "Your eyes got all sad."

He slid his hand over one of hers and pulled it away so he could kiss her palm. "You read me so well."

"Of course, I do. You do the same with me. I can't seem to hide a damn thing from you."

He kissed her cheek and sighed. "Fun tonight, Tessa. Just fun."

She leaned forward and kissed his shoulder. "Got it. Now, go and try to get that ball of yours into that hole. We're in the middle of a competition, Gallagher, and you're losing." She smacked his butt slightly and grinned. "Onward, noble steed!"

Murphy snorted and went back to his position. At this rate, they would never finish the game—not that he minded. He just liked spending time with Tessa outside of the house and all the drama that came with their lives.

"You sound like Rowan when you say that." He kept his concentration on the ball, and this time, hit it right into the hole. "Hell yeah."

Tessa laughed. "Rowan is a hoot, and yeah, that did sound like something she'd say. And hole in two? I think I'd better step up my game, Gallagher."

He winked before whistling and headed over to pick up his ball. "Better watch out, Stone. I play for keeps."

"Game on."

"WHO KNEW miniature golf could get you so horny?" Tessa panted as she went to her knees in front of him. They'd barely made it into the house before she had his back to the door and his cock in her hands.

Seriously, he had to be the luckiest man alive when it came to Tessa. The rest of his life might be going to shit, but Tessa? She made life worth living.

Again, he wasn't going to think about the ramifications of that statement, and since she had her lips on the tip of his dick, it was pretty hard to think about anything.

"Jesus Christ, Tessa." He wrapped his hand in her hair and pumped his hips, her mouth a warm caress on his cock. "And it wasn't the golf. It was that little shake you did with your hips when you hit the ball just right and the way you bent over right in front of me, brushing that luscious ass of yours over my groin when you'd reach down and get your ball." His eyes crossed when she sucked hard, and he let out a shaky breath. "Holy fuck. Keep going."

She let him go with a wet pop and licked her lips. "You were just as bad with all those brushes and caresses. I'm pretty sure I soaked through my panties."

He growled and lifted her up before she could suck on him again. "I need to be inside you. *Now.*"

He had his mouth on her, and his hand inside her panties in the next instant. She sucked in a breath even as she clung to him when he speared her with two fingers. She was so damn wet, he slid in easily, her damp heat squeezing him hard.

"You're close, aren't you, baby?"

She nodded, rocking her hips so her clit brushed his hand. "I need to come, Murphy. Please. I need you."

He bit her lip, and she gasped. "Rock on my hand. Keep going. Make yourself come."

She shook her head. "I want you to do it. I can make myself come with just my hands and my vibrator, but when you do it? I come even harder. So hard that my nipples ache and my body shakes. Make me come, Murphy."

He kissed her again, moving her back so her butt rested along the edge of the couch. "Since you're begging, baby." He went to his knees in front of her and stripped her out of her shorts in one quick motion. Then he had his mouth on her cunt, his tongue flicking her clit and his fingers pumping in and out of her.

One leg wrapped around his shoulder and the other pressed to his chest as she shook. She slid one hand into his hair, tugging, and he didn't care. He just needed her to come on his face, needed her to lose control so he could taste every inch of her.

There was nothing better than the taste of Tessa Stone when she came.

She made a soft sound, just a catch of breath, and he knew she was close. So he twisted his fingers just right, and she bucked against him, coming so hard that he had to keep one hand on her hip so she wouldn't fall.

"Inside me," she gasped. "I need you inside me."

He kissed her, loving the way she moaned at the taste of herself on his tongue. "You're a greedy lover tonight."

"I just had my mouth on your dick *and* had to keep my

teeth safe from that piercing. I deserve your cock, mister. So give it to me."

He gave her a mock sigh before shucking off his jeans after pulling out a condom from his pocket. "Take off your shirt and bra, baby. I'm going to need to see those tits when I fuck you."

She licked her lips. "I want to see your chest, too."

He slowly rolled the condom down his length and nodded. "Can do." He stripped off his shirt and groaned when she slid her bra off, and her breasts bounced. Her nipples were swollen and red, ready for him.

"Have I mentioned that I love that you have such sensitive nipples?" he cupped one breast and slid the pad of his thumb over her rigid peak. She shivered, moaning.

"I could come like that, but I don't want to." Her eyes pleaded with him. "Please. Inside."

He winked and moved closer before gripping her hips and lifting her so her butt rested on the edge of the couch. "That I can do." Then he thrust into her hard with one movement, and both of them froze.

"Holy shit," she breathed. "Did you get bigger?"

"You say the sweetest things, baby." He kissed the tip of her nose. "I mean, seriously. If I'm ever having a bad day, I just need you to talk to my dick and I'd be squared for a few hours."

She let out a laugh, and he joined her. "How can I be laughing with your dick all hard and yummy inside me."

He reached between them and slid his thumb over her

clit, loving the way her eyes rolled back. "Because this isn't just sex. This is you and me. We laugh. We fuck. We fight. We fuck again. But it's fucking with everything else that comes with it." He cupped the back of her head so their gazes met. "Just you and me, baby. That's all we need."

She bit her lip, an emotion in her eyes he couldn't quite place before she *moved*. "Yes," she hissed as he started to move with her.

Though they'd started out fast and had laughed through it all, this part was anything but. It was all slow movements and arches, feeling every inch of each other. He'd never made love to a woman before, and he thought this just might be it, but he wasn't ready to call it that. Not yet, not when he didn't know what was next.

But as they came, their bodies sweaty and wrapped around one another, Murphy knew that they'd never be the same. And even thinking they'd be able to walk away from this unchanged would have been a lie. Tessa was in his pores, in his skin...and if something altered that, he wasn't sure what he'd do.

15

Dating wasn't going to kill Tessa, but prepping for the date just might. Murphy wouldn't tell her where they were going, only that she could dress casually, and he would be the one driving. Considering most guys wanted to drive anyway, she wasn't sure why he'd even mentioned the latter. Somehow, she was about to go on her first real date with Murphy. They'd had sex, sure, had even gone to play miniature golf. And considering that they were living in the same house, they ate meals together often, but going out with him tonight would be a little different. Or maybe a whole lot different.

"Are you ready to go?" Murphy leaned in her doorway, his hands in his pockets and a small grin on his face. He looked a little better than he had that morning, considering he'd had dark circles under his eyes from not sleeping and she'd forced him to take a nap. She hadn't let any of his brothers wake him up with their texts or phone calls like they had been prone to do recently. Everyone was so worried about Murphy; sometimes, they forgot that most days he just needed rest. She was guilty of that herself and hadn't wanted to leave the house tonight as it was. She had offered just to stay in, but he hadn't wanted his *girlfriend* to not have a real date.

His girlfriend.

How on earth had that happened? She wasn't sure, but she couldn't help the warm feeling sliding through her even as she panicked a bit. She'd only had one serious relationship in her life, and it hadn't ended well. Hell, it had ended with a restraining order and bruises on more than just her heart, but Murphy wasn't her ex, and she needed to keep remembering that. It was just hard to put herself out there sometimes. The one time she'd thought she was good enough for the perfect man her parents might approve of, she'd ended up picking the worst man of all.

Murphy wasn't like him, and that was the one thing she could cling to when she got nervous about how quickly they were getting serious. Not that either of them talked about their future together more than wanting to go out in public and be a *real* couple, but that was still a lot more serious than anything she'd had before. She wasn't going to date anyone else when she was with Murphy, and she knew he was the same way with her. This was nothing like Brent and whatever they'd had.

This was Murphy.

This was important.

And this was scary as all hell.

"Tessa? You're in your head again." Murphy walked toward her, and she shook her head, annoyed with herself for letting her thoughts go off on yet another tangent. When he cupped her face with his palm, she leaned into his hand, enjoying the heat of him, the feel of him.

"Sorry, I just have a lot on my mind. But I think I'm ready to go." She looked down at her stylishly ripped jeans that went right above her ankle boots that also had a very high heel on them. She'd put on layered silk tanks with a couple of necklaces and a short jacket in case anywhere they went had too much air conditioning. All in all, she just needed a fedora, and she'd suddenly be a twenty-something hipster, but it sort of worked as an ensemble.

Murphy's gaze traveled the length of her body up to where her cleavage peeked out of her lacy bra above the tanks' necklines and into her eyes. "You look fucking sexy as hell, and it's taking everything in me not to strip you out of those clothes and fuck you hard on your dresser. But, I promised you a night out, and we are going to do that. But when we get home, I'll fuck you on the dresser, maybe bend you over the edge of the bed, and eat you out a couple times just for good measure."

She snorted a laugh even as her thighs trembled at his words. The man could seriously make her wet just by talking. Now that was some serious talent.

"Are you sure we can't just get to all of that now and skip

the date? I'm sure you'll be a wonderful date, but I really like your penis, and I'd like to get to know him a little bit better."

Murphy barked out a laugh and put his hands on her hips to bring her forward. She could feel the hard lines of his rigid cock pressed against her stomach, and it was all she could do to hold back a moan. She seriously couldn't get enough of this man, and she had to remind herself that they were taking things slowly. Murphy's own body was trying to hurt him, and she'd be damned if she hurt him, too.

"I'm taking you out on a date, damn it. Then we'll fuck until we're exhausted and can sleep the rest of the weekend away. Are you going to be okay walking for a bit in those shoes? I forgot to say we might be walking tonight."

She frowned, disappointed and pleased at his words since he seemed to want her as much as she wanted him, before looking down at her heeled boots. "I own higher heels, and because these are boots with a slight wedge, they're actually a lot more comfortable than some of the pumps I own. How much walking are we talking about? Can't you just tell me where we're going? Then I'll decide if I need to change shoes."

Murphy let out a breath before kissing her softly. Damn, she loved his kisses. "We're going to one of my favorite breweries to take a tour. There are free samples along the way and a lot more samples at the end for us. Plus...pretzels. I mean, what more do you need besides beer and pretzels?"

"But you can't drink. How much fun can you have not being able to drink on a brewery tour?" Though the idea sounded right up her alley, and she couldn't help but think of the last tour she'd done. That winery with Brent had *so* not been her thing, but this? This was pure Murphy and Tessa.

Murphy tucked a piece of her hair behind her ear and gave her one of those soft smiles that she knew was dangerous. Because the more he looked like that, the more she was certain she was going to fall in love with him. And she wasn't sure how she felt about that.

"One of us would need to drive anyway; unless we took a cab or one of those car services. And all I really want to do is be with you while we go learn about how beer is made and what flavors they're making today and what their favorite IPA is."

"Neither of us like IPAs, and we both talked about the fact that we can't wait till this trend is done."

"Be that as it may, it'll still be fun, even if all I get to do is eat pretzels and have some other nonalcoholic beers. You never know, they could actually be good this time."

Tessa gave him a cautious look but nodded. "As long as you're fine with that, I think it sounds fun. And you know beer and pretzels are kind of my favorite thing."

Murphy leaned forward and licked her bottom lip, sending shivers down her spine. "What about Jell-O?"

She swallowed hard, wanting him more now than she ever had before. "Jell-O's up there, too."

Murphy kissed her again. "Good." He cleared his throat. "Now, really, those shoes? You going to be okay?"

She nodded. "Yep. Though you might have to rub my feet when we get home." It was still weird to her that she kept saying "home" in relation to Murphy, but she wasn't going to go there.

He winced. "Feet? I don't know, babe. Feet are kind of weird."

She smacked him lightly on the arm and rolled her eyes. "Then no eating me out. Sorry. I know it's your favorite thing."

"Damn right, it's my favorite thing. I love being between your legs, sucking your clit and licking your cream. I want to bite and taste every inch of you, bury my face in that sweet pussy until you come hard, squeezing those thighs around my head. Eating pussy is not just for you, babe. I *love* it. I take my time and make sure you come, don't I?"

As she was about to come right then just thinking about it, she could only nod. "Uh, we should go before I make my panties any wetter."

Murphy groaned and adjusted himself behind his zipper. "Yeah, driving with a hard-on isn't easy."

She winked and reached out to cup him over his jeans. "I know, baby, I know. Don't worry, though, I'll take care of you and Little Murphy."

"Damn right, you will." She squeezed, and he groaned. "And I'll rub your feet because you're worth it."

"And not just because of my mouth?" she asked, laughing.

"Well, your mouth is part of it for sure, but I really like the rest of you, too." He kissed her again, then took her hand off his crotch and led her out of her bedroom. "And we're going to be late if we keep fucking around in here. As much as I love dirty talk, it's making me sweat."

She fanned herself and laughed, picking up her cross-body purse on the way out. "You're not the only one. Whew." Grateful they were headed toward his car and finally getting out of the house, she let her thoughts wander. She was falling in love with him so hard and so fast, she could barely keep up, but she knew if she dwelled on that, she'd only make things worse.

Just for tonight, she thought. *Just live for tonight.* That was all she could do.

"I MIGHT ACTUALLY BE TOO STUFFED," Tessa said, eyeing the free pilsner staring at her. "How many pretzels did we eat?"

Murphy let out a groan and wrapped his arm around her shoulders over the chair. "I think too many. And then however many chips, and the mini burgers, and those onion rings. I didn't realize they'd added a whole dinner and appetizer section to the Saturday night tour. I think I ate enough for four people."

"I'm pretty sure I ate the same amount as you did, and now I don't think I'm going to be able to roll myself to the car to get home." She leaned on him, resting her head on his shoulder. They'd spent the evening eating and drinking their way through the history of the brewery and beer making in general. She'd really enjoyed the chemistry part of it and had made Murphy laugh hysterically when she'd told him that. Though she had known him for what seemed like forever now, they were still learning more and more about each other.

Now, they were sitting at one of the tables outside the café area and were relatively alone. Others were either heading home or finding more food and drinks to indulge in. Tessa wasn't sure how they were all doing it. She was past stuffed, and really just enjoying sitting with Murphy and talking.

"So, this isn't the first time you've taken this tour?" Tessa asked after a while.

"I took it once before with my brothers after I turned twenty-one. So it's been a few years. They'd wanted to take me *on* my twenty-first birthday, but mom passed away right around then."

Tessa squeezed his thigh but didn't say anything, letting him finish out his thoughts.

"I think she was just so exhausted. Though they said it was a brain aneurysm, I figure it started because she hadn't really been taking care of herself. She took care of me for so long. Dad died only a short time later. A heart attack at his age." There was a tone of sadness in his voice that pulled at Tessa and made her want to gather him up in her arms and never let go. But she knew he wouldn't have appreciated that right then.

"It's not your fault, you know. And it's not your fault now if we all want to make sure we take care of you." The words were spoken quietly, but she knew he had heard them.

"Most parts of me know. Some days are a little harder than others."

"I never knew my real father. He was a drugged-out mess that had left my mom before I could even walk. My mom wasn't much better. I probably would've been better off if she had left me, too. In the end, she overdosed, and I almost starved as a four-year-old in our crappy one-bedroom apartment in the worst part of town. I only remember things in patches, and even then, sometimes I think they're just glimpses from movies and books rather than memories of my birth parents. Grace and Chris took me into their home two days after the police found me. They started the adoption paperwork right then, not even waiting to see if I would fit into their household. I still don't know how I ended up so lucky in the end. Grace and Chris are my parents. They're the best things that have ever happened to me. And I almost fucked it all up because I didn't know what to do with it."

She hadn't meant to say all that and wasn't sure why she had. Only Liz knew exactly what had happened when she'd been a kid who didn't care and an unruly and ungrateful teenager. But Murphy had shared something that scared him deep down, and she knew he deserved at least that much from her. She couldn't tell herself that she was slowly falling in love with him, and yet keep the most personal parts of herself hidden.

Murphy kissed the top of her head. "From what I saw when I met your parents, they seem like wonderful people. I'm glad you have them. I'm glad that they were there for you. I don't want to think about what could have happened if they hadn't been there."

Tessa nodded and swallowed hard. "I wasn't grateful at first. Or rather, I didn't know how to be grateful. I was such a stupid shit. When I was a little kid, I think I was so scared that someone would take me away that I tried too hard to be perfect. Then, somehow, I got it into my head that I needed to test them or something. So I started smoking. I had sex far too young. I started shoplifting stupid shit like gum. I skipped school, and I talked back to my teachers and my parents. I was just a horrible, horrible kid. And Grace and Chris never deserved a single moment of it. They didn't let me get away with anything that they caught, and I know that was the right decision. I was grounded, forced to see counselors, and Grace and Chris tried to talk to me and figure out what was wrong. Yet I still fucked things up."

Tessa closed her eyes, remembering the disappointment on her parents' faces, but they had never given up on her. Not once.

She'd been so damn lucky—and so damn clueless.

"I got arrested for stealing makeup that I didn't even like, and I think that was the final straw. They told me that they loved me and that they knew I was hurting, but that I couldn't continue on that path. They were going to home-school me and get me away from the people that kept pulling me down, and told me that they would do all in their power to make me realize I was loved."

She wiped at a tear, and Murphy squeezed her tightly.

"Then I got arrested again when I was sixteen for drinking. Only this time, they didn't come and pick me up. I thought they'd finally given up on me." She swallowed back her tears. "It turned out they'd gotten into a car accident on the way to the station to pick me up and deal with things, and Grace had fractured her collarbone thanks to the seatbelt."

"Oh, baby."

"That was a turning point for me because I wasn't just hurting myself anymore. She wouldn't have been on the road, and the driver who dropped his sandwich on his lap and ended up in the wrong lane wouldn't have hit my parents if it hadn't been for me."

"Babe." One word and she knew what Murphy was thinking.

"I know it wasn't totally my fault, but I was partially to blame. Anyway, I cleaned up my act after that. I had to. I went to school—a new school with new friends because I wasn't doing well at the other one frankly—and I excelled. I didn't drink, or smoke, or do anything stupid like I had before. I swore off boys. I got into college after taking a gap year at a community college to up my grades, and I was doing well...until I met my ex." She couldn't even say his name without bile filling her throat, so she didn't even bother.

Murphy's arm tightened around her again before he turned so they faced each other. "What happened?"

She winced, not knowing exactly how much he knew about her folks. They'd talked some, but she wasn't sure. "You know my parents come from money, right? And that they've earned even more by being cautious and hard-working?"

He nodded. "I know a little from what you've told me and from seeing the plans they want for the house."

"Okay, so my parents are so not like rich people from the movies with yachts and not wearing white after labor day and all that jazz. But some of their friends are. And one of those friends had a nephew." She pinched the bridge of her nose. "He was from Denver but not near me, so I hadn't known him when he was younger. We met in college, and I thought he was the dreamiest guy ever. Andy was bright, sweet, caring, handsome, and totally fit in with what I thought my parents wanted me to have."

"What did he do?" Murphy asked, his voice tight.

"He started to try and control my life. He thought I would be the perfect Mrs. to his Mr., and that wasn't some-thing I was thinking of at that time. I was in college, and my best friend was Liz. So we worked our behinds off to get amazing grades so we could go into the next phase of our educations and then get kickass jobs. That was my plan, and yet Andy wanted to derail that. It started off slowly but got worse over time. He started yelling and acting like a completely different person."

She paused.

"Then he hit me."

Murphy's eyes went dark. "Did you hit him back and call the cops?"

She couldn't help but smile and cup his face. "I didn't hit him back. He only hurt me the once, but it was bad enough that I couldn't fight back. I called the cops and my parents, and there was a restraining order put in place after I filed charges. But because of family money and the fact that he'd never done anything wrong before in his life blah blah blah...he got off with just a warning that he couldn't be near me."

"I want to find this bastard and kick his ass. That scum-fucker doesn't deserve to be outside of jail."

Tessa kissed Murphy then, feeling a weight lift off her chest for the first time in forever. "Thank you. I didn't mean to tell you all of that tonight. I kind of wanted to slowly tell you a bit of where I came from, but it all rushed out."

He slid his hands down her shoulders, so gently that she knew he was thinking of what her ex had done. "I'm glad you felt that you could tell me." He kissed her with a bare brush of lips. "Now I think we should go because the place is closing and I just want to hold you, okay?"

She pulled back and looked around and noticed that the

lights were indeed dimming and people were cleaning up. "Oh, wow, we've been out here awhile."

"I don't mind," he said with a soft smile. "Let's get you home."

Tessa took his hand and leaned into him as they walked to his car. She'd never opened up to another man like she had with Murphy, and yet knowing that she had to him told her so much more about what she felt about him than anything else she could have done.

But when Murphy froze beside her, she froze, as well, ice creeping down her spine.

"What the fuck?" he growled.

Tessa blinked, not quite sure what she was seeing. There were still at least a dozen cars in the parking lot, but only one had all four tires slashed, and a window knocked out.

Murphy's.

"Oh, God," she sputtered. "What the hell?"

"I'm calling the cops," Murphy growled. "Fucking punks. Come on, we're going inside where I can keep you safe." She let him lead her toward the building as he called the police, but she couldn't help but look behind her.

No other car in the parking lot had damage. Only his. But why? It didn't make any sense, and she didn't have the answers. All she did have was the need to hold Murphy close because something was going on.

She just had no idea what it was.

16

M urphy was oddly elated yet fearful for his appointment, and that didn't make for an easy stomach. His cancer didn't have a cure—few did—but his treatment plan was much different than those he'd heard of before everything had happened this summer. He only had to deal with a few weeks of taking a pill that would try to combat the attacking cells in his body. Then, he just needed blood transfusions to make sure he had enough energy to keep going.

Today was his last chemo day of this round of treatments, and would hopefully be the last chemo day ever. He would still have to come back to the clinic every week for a little while to get his blood checked to ensure his stability until his check-ins could be tapered off to once a month and then maybe even less.

Tessa wrapped her arms around him from behind, and

he leaned into her hold. They were standing outside of the clinic and had been for a few minutes. Tessa hadn't said a word, she'd just taken his hand and leaned into him. Now, he was the one using her for strength. When all of this had started, he never would've thought he'd have Tessa by his side for some of the scariest parts of his life. Now, he honestly didn't know what he would've done if she weren't there. She wasn't only his roommate, or the woman he was sleeping with, or even just his girlfriend, she was becoming something far more.

Right then, however, he couldn't dwell on that and think about how it made him feel. He needed to get through today and what it all meant, and then he could start thinking about a future. When someone tells you that your life is going to be forever changed and that you might not have that much of a life at all, it's hard to put everything into perspective. Murphy had been spending most of his time trying to figure out how to get healthy rather than thinking about what could happen if he didn't. He'd needed a distraction from the idea that this might not work, but Tessa hadn't been it. If anything, she had been the one to make him focus.

"Murph?" Her voice had gone soft as if she were afraid she'd spook him. She wasn't wrong.

"Sorry." He rubbed his hands over hers and tugged on her wrist, so she moved to stand in front of him. He slid his hands through her hair and rested his forehead on hers. He just needed her touch, her presence to center himself. He didn't know when that had happened. When had he grown to rely on her for more than a laugh and a heated glance? Regardless, he wasn't as scared of the possibilities as he once had been.

"I'd ask what's on your mind, but I can probably guess."

Probably not...

She shifted and kissed his chest, and he wrapped his arms around her, tugging her close. Did she care about him as much as he cared about her? He wasn't sure he wanted to know the answer. She'd been hurt in the past, and he knew coming back from that hadn't been easy. He didn't know what she wanted from him in the end, and wasn't sure what would happen when the dust settled and she realized that they were not only a couple but also living together. He spent more time in her bed than his, and yet they hadn't discussed it. There just had been too much going on in their lives with the move, his treatments, her work, the incident at the brewery that they still didn't have answers for, and their slow turn into something more as a couple.

"Let's get you inside," she whispered. "The faster we get you in there, the sooner we can get you out, right?" She gave him a sad smile, and he kissed the edge of her mouth.

"That's one way to look at it," he agreed. "And the way that I've usually been going about it." He pulled back slightly and rubbed his chest, a little more sore today than he had been earlier in the week. The treatment was taking a lot out of him, and he wasn't working as many hours as usual, but his body was still taking a hit. "I just...I have this weird feeling, you know?"

Her eyes widened, and her hands tightened on his hips. "What do you mean?"

"I don't know...I just...I can't explain it other than I don't know if I want to go in there."

She pressed her lips together before blowing out a breath. "It's just one more pill and a check-up today, Murphy. That's it. You can do it. Then we can go home, and I can cuddle you before I need to head into work. How does that sound?"

He rubbed his cheek on the top of her head and sighed. "Sounds like I should get in there and get it over with."

Tessa pulled back and cupped his face. "If I could do this for you, I would. If I could take some of your burden, I would. It's not fair that this keeps happening to you. It's not fair that so much is out of our hands. But I'm going to sit right next to you and hold your hand during this last part. Liz already assured me that I could have one of those folding chairs so you wouldn't be alone. So anything you need from me? It's yours. If you need to scream, shout, be angry at something, I'm here for that, too. I'm here, Murphy. I'm here."

He loved this woman. Loved her more than he could say. And one day soon, he'd find a way to tell her.

"You...you are amazing." He kissed her then, just soft enough that it was a bare brush rather than a full kiss.

"I try," she said with a smile that didn't quite reach her

eyes. She'd been off since they'd found the tires slashed on his truck, and for some reason, he thought she blamed herself. He'd tried to make her feel better, but she'd waved him off. They were both in their own heads so much recently, it was a wonder they could even stand here like this at all.

"Okay, you two," Liz said as she walked out of the front door and out toward them. "I've been watching y'all for ten minutes now—as have most of the people in the waiting room—and while you're both adorable, and I wish I'd thought to bring my camera out here for a photo, you need to get in here."

Liz had tried to sound stern when she spoke, but Murphy had seen the softness in her expression.

"Let's do this." He gripped Tessa's hand, and they made their way into the clinic, a sense of urgency pounding through his blood more than before.

By the time he got through the paperwork and was in his chair, Max was already there, with Abby sitting beside him on one of those folding chairs. The staff had set up another chair for Tessa by Murphy as each of the treatment chairs were filled with patients needing one therapy or another.

"Full house," Max said with a grin. "I think they're here just to throw you a party."

Murphy sank into the chair and snorted. "Sounds festive."

"We try," one of the older women said from her chair on

the other side of the room. She'd been in there a few times at the same time as Murphy, but he didn't know much about her other than that her name was Ester.

Murphy smiled despite their setting and let his nurse start his IV since he needed fluids that day. Tessa took his free hand and leaned into his chair. This was the first time she'd come into the clinic with him like this, and while before he hadn't thought he needed anyone by his side, he knew he was wrong.

He *needed* Tessa.

And not just for today.

"So, what's on your agenda after this?" Max asked, his free hand twined with Abby's. She had her other hand on her small baby bump and was also leaning into Max's chair like Tessa was. "Maybe a cruise? Or a big dinner?"

Murphy snorted. "Those two things are kind of on opposite ends of the scale."

"True, but I wanted to cover my bases."

"I was thinking more of a nap. A long one." He glanced at Tessa and winked. She didn't blush or hide; instead, she rolled her eyes and gave him a look that spoke volumes.

"All by yourself so you can rest and rejuvenate. Understandable. I'll be sure to leave you *alone* in bed for the next week or so just in case." She kept her face expressionless, and he couldn't help but smile.

"You wouldn't do that." He leaned down and whispered so only she could hear. "You like my dick too much."

She whispered right back. "I have a very nice vibrator and dildo set. I'm good."

Murphy closed his eyes and pictured her using those on herself to make herself come, and he had to hold in a groan.

"If you aren't careful, you're going to need an extra blood transfusion since everything you have seems to be going to Little Murphy right now," Tessa said dryly, her voice low— just not low enough apparently.

A few of the other patients started laughing, and Tessa's eyes widened. But instead of blushing, she just raised her chin and smirked at Murphy.

"Well, it's true," she defended, and that set everyone off again.

"It's good to see you like this," Max put in once the din had died down. "We need laughter in a room like this. Most days, we just sit here and not talk to one another and pretend that everything's going to be okay. Yeah, everything damn well better be okay, but it's nice to see that sometimes it can be."

Murphy studied his friend from childhood that had become an even better friend now. He didn't know how Max did it every day, with what was racing through his system, but the man always had a positive head on his shoulders. He did everything he could every day to strive to be a better person for his fiancée and for their unborn child. Seeing Max be who he was with such a careless grace had perhaps changed the way Murphy saw his own disease. If Max could be this kind of person despite everything coming at him, maybe Murphy could try to be something similar. He had to credit Max and some of the other patients in this room for just *being*. Without seeing them strive for a better life even while sick, Murphy wasn't sure he would have done everything he'd done over these past few weeks. He had fallen for his best friend and roommate because he'd given himself that chance. Had things not gone as they did, he might have been too worried about the consequences of what *could* happen if things went wrong to continue, and would have stayed far away, doing nothing because he thought that it was a safer option. He had been wrong for as long as he had known Tessa because he hadn't let her be a part of his life.

Maybe it was the fact that he was staring down his own mortality that he kept thinking about what people in his life truly meant to him. Without his brothers and their wives and husband, Murphy knew he wouldn't be the same man today. He had gone into this whole experience being scared. But looking at his sickness as a journey to get through, he could see an end in sight and something he could live for, rather than an end to the journey he couldn't escape. Because of the cancer, the timing of everything had accelerated to the point where he still wasn't sure that the fact that he *had* cancer again to begin with had even truly hit him yet. He was just going day by day, trying to get healthy, trying to keep his family in the loop without harming them in the process. He tried to keep working and looking at his business as something he could be part of for years to come. And he tried to see himself in the future with a woman he hadn't let himself fall in love with until he had broken down the barriers that had kept him safe and alone for so long.

And maybe all of this was just a little too much, and his chemo was making him hallucinate to the point where he was having some very deep thoughts that should've scared him and yet only pushed him to keep going. To fight. To live.

"We all need a reason to smile. Every damn day."

Tessa squeezed his hand, and he turned to her. "You need to introduce me to Abby," she whispered fiercely. "We've only seen each other in passing, and now it's awkward."

He winced, pulling his thoughts out of self-revelation and into the present, then he turned to Max. "I think we kind of forgot to introduce our women to each other."

"Our women?" Tessa, asked her voice rising at the end. "Caveman much?"

Murphy let out a small growl. "Be quiet, woman, before I pull your hair and drag you off to my cave later."

She fluttered her lashes. "Oh, really? How dreamy? I've always wanted a big, bad caveman to knock me over the head and treat me like a little woman." He knew she was joking considering that he never really acted like a controlling jackass around her, but she had also been through hell with her ex, so he had to tread lightly. "Anyway, hi, Abby, I'm Tessa, Murphy's girlfriend. I saw you out in the waiting room a couple of times, but I really didn't know if you were Max's wife or not."

Abby waved from her seat, not letting go of Max's hand. "Hi, it's good to finally actually meet you, Tessa. Max's been talking to me about you from what he knows from Murphy and what he's seen himself when you've been around the clinic. I'm glad that we're both here today to celebrate Murphy's last treatment."

"I hope the boys have been telling you good things," Tessa said wryly. "I'd hate to have to start kicking."

"I bruise, baby, be gentle." Murphy lifted their joined hands and pressed a kiss to her skin.

She rolled her eyes. "I always am." She paused. "Well, only if you ask nicely."

The others in the room laughed again, and Murphy relaxed into the chair, feeling as though he were hanging out with friends, not waiting for the drugs in his body to fight the cancer that had tried to take over.

He should have known something would happen to change it all.

He should have fucking known.

Max and Abby talked about their upcoming wedding as Tessa added bits of advice that she'd picked up from helping plan Liz's. Liz herself came in to check on everyone a few times, along with Murphy's nurse. They were busy that day, so Murphy didn't have time to stop and chat with Liz.

A sense of foreboding crawled up Murphy's spine as he looked at Max and frowned. The other man was rubbing his chest, a grimace on his face as he blinked quickly. Max looked over at Murphy, his eyes wide before he turned back to Abby. Max's fiancée's smile fell as she stared at the other man before she stood up, her face pale.

"Max?" she said quietly, her voice a rasp.

Murphy's friend didn't respond.

"Max? Max!" Abby shook Max's shoulders, but the other man just slumped down.

"Liz!" Murphy called out, practically screaming. Tessa was on her feet and running out of the room before he could even look at her, and Murphy tried to unhook himself from his IV so he could help his friend. Not that he knew what he could do, but he couldn't just fucking *sit* there when something was wrong.

The others in the room were either trying to do the same as he was or looking as shell-shocked as he felt.

This couldn't be happening.

This couldn't be fucking happening.

Doctors, nurses, and staff rushed into the room at that moment, Tessa on their heels. They surrounded Max, blocking Murphy's view. Someone came over to Murphy's chair and checked his IV in his arm while unhooking it from the lounger.

"We need the space," the young nurse said. Maybe she was a nurse, perhaps she was a lab tech. He honestly didn't know, but he stood up with Tessa by his side and went to stand by another chair so those who knew what they were doing could help.

"What's going on?" he asked, his voice was hoarse.

"Let them work, Mr. Gallagher. Just remain calm so you don't hurt yourself."

Murphy went numb, his body no longer hot or cold...it just *was*.

Tessa gripped his hands, but she hadn't said a thing. Her face had gone so pale he thought she might be sick, but she didn't stay anything. She just stared blankly at where the staff tried to work on Max.

Things moved quickly after that. Somehow, there were enough people on hand to move everyone out of the room and into other parts of the clinic where they could continue their treatments. One of the nurses had pulled out Murphy's IV since he was finished, but he didn't leave the spot where he stood. His body ached, and his stomach turned violently, but he couldn't *move*.

Then the sound of a keening wail hit his ears, and everything went blank.

Abby.

That was Abby.

"That poor girl," Ester from her seat beside Murphy and Tessa. "Life just isn't fair to the young ones."

Someone else said something, but Murphy couldn't hear them. He could only focus on the door in front of him and pray that it was all a mistake. Max had just been smiling and laughing with them.

He couldn't be dead.

He *couldn't*.

Then Liz walked through the doorway, her eyes shiny,

and her mouth set in a firm line. When she shook her head, Murphy needed to sit down. His world crashed from beneath his feet, and the reality of what had just happened and what could *still* happen smashed into him.

Max was dead.

Abby was breaking.

Murphy was still here.

And Tessa? He looked over at the woman he loved and tried to figure out what to say, but she just stood next to him, her arms wrapped around her middle as she listened to Abby's cries. She hadn't said a word, and Murphy wasn't sure there was anything to say.

Cancer had taken another victim.

And Murphy was still here.

What kind of fairness was that?

17

Death wasn't supposed to be pretty. It wasn't supposed to be pure. But Tessa had thought it would be *something*. Knowing the end had come to someone she'd begun to truly like and admire should have done something to her body, right? To her mind? She should have felt grief or fear or hate or sadness or *something*.

Instead, she was just numb.

Murphy's friend from childhood, the same friend who had been there through all of Murphy's illnesses was gone, and there was nothing anyone could do.

Abby would have to have their baby without Max. She'd have to raise their child without its father. She'd never get her wedding after all this time.

Max was gone.

And Tessa had no idea what to do.

"Tessa?"

Murphy's voice brought her out of her thoughts and back into the present. They had come home soon after Liz had walked into the room to let them know that Max had passed away. Though Liz hadn't been able to say what had happened to Max, Tessa was sure they would find out soon.

"Yes?" Her voice sounded crisp, short, and she was pretty sure that it had been the first time she'd spoken since she'd run from the room to tell Liz that something was wrong with Max.

Murphy gave her a weird look and looked down at his phone. "Abby just texted." He swallowed hard, and Tessa told herself to go to him but she couldn't. She was so damned *scared*. "They think Max had a blood clot that moved to his heart, and his heart was already weak from all the shit they've put into his body over the years."

Murphy didn't add that he too had gone through similar treatments.

That he too could get a blood clot.

That he could leave her with just a gasp of breath and a set of wide eyes on a pale face.

"They'll know more later, and Abby said she'd tell us if we wanted to know, but yeah...a fucking blood clot. It's a danger to all of us on the meds we're on, but most of us put that thought aside, you know? Because no matter what, we're still going to fight. As long as we can, at least. We're facing *cancer,* so the idea that a blood clot can take us seems so arbitrary. Fuck, Tessa. I can't believe he's gone."

Tessa didn't say anything, she wasn't sure she could.

"Tessa?" Murphy's voice sounded closer, and she forced herself to look up to find him standing in front of her. They weren't touching, but they were close enough to do so easily if they reached out.

Only neither of them did.

"Max died," she whispered, her voice hollow. "How... why is that right? Why did he have to die?" She blinked up at him, tears finally stinging her eyes. "I keep asking myself these questions, and yet in the back of my mind, all I can do is be thankful that it wasn't you today. How horrible am I? A man is dead, and all I can think about is the fact that you aren't. Max isn't going to watch his child be born. He's not going to be there for everything that happens in that child's life. Abby isn't going to be able to say her vows and be with the man she loves. Ever. All that is gone in the blink of an eye, and yet some part of me knows we should have been thinking about an outcome like this the whole time. He had cancer. *You* have cancer. You could leave me, leave us, and it would be out of your control. Everything just seems out of our control. And yet all I can do right now is be happy that it wasn't you. What kind of monster feels happiness that someone else is dead? Maybe it's not happiness. Maybe it's relief. And, somehow, that feels even worse. A man died, and all I can do is think about how you are here, yet you could've been the one to die."

Tessa closed her eyes, putting her hands over her face so she wouldn't have to look into Murphy's eyes after she'd rambled all the horrid things going through her mind. And the thing was, she hadn't even been aware she'd been feeling those things until she blurted it all out for him to hear. She wouldn't be surprised if he packed up and left her right then.

And frankly, she wouldn't blame him.

With those words, she'd become the person she hated once again, the person she'd thought she had buried down deep after her mom had gotten hurt because of her. Apparently, she hadn't grown up much, after all. She was still the same Tessa that hurt others because she was afraid of being hurt.

Only she was hurting right now, and she had no idea what to do about it.

Murphy reached out and cupped her face. "You aren't a horrible person." He swallowed hard, and she saw the sheen in his eyes. Damn it, he couldn't cry, or she wouldn't make it. "Baby, none of us were expecting what happened, and however you're feeling is okay. We all respond to grief differently, and if your response that you figured out what you're feeling for me and that you want me to be part of your life, that's okay, too. None of us are perfect, Tessa. We are human. We are fragile. That's why we were at the clinic today. I don't think it's sunk in yet that Max is gone. He just came back into my life, and I had thought we would be able to survive together. I don't know what's coming next, but whatever it is, I don't want to do it without you."

Tears were falling freely down Tessa's cheeks now. She wasn't numb anymore. "I was so scared. I'm still scared. I just found you. I just let you in. I just figured out what kind of man you are and how much you mean to me. I should have known that far earlier than this. I don't know what I would do if I lost you, Murphy." She was baring her soul to him, and she prayed that he would understand; that he would take what she had to give and find a way to make it work.

"I'm scared, too. I'm scared every damn day that somehow this is going to be my last. I was scared even before I found the bruises. I spent so much of my life early on just trying to have another day that I forgot to figure out who Murphy is. Then, when I finally started to figure that out, life hit me upside the head again. Or maybe not life. Maybe that was fate just reminding me that sometimes you have to look backward before you can move forward. I'm scared every time I have to work, and I find out that I'm not strong enough to be the Gallagher I was before this. I'm scared every time I go into the clinic that they'll say that the cancer is worse and that my treatments have to get harsher and even more complicated. I'm scared that because my body doesn't look like I'm going through chemo and that cancer's inside me, I'm going to forget to fight. And then I'm scared that I'm putting everything into a single word: fight, while those who lose their lives to cancer fought just as hard as I did. I'm scared because it's not a matter of fighting, it's a matter of medicine and luck, and everything else is out of our control. Through it all, though, I'm scared that I'm not going to have you by my side. Hell, I'm scared how much I need you by my side. You fell into my life at the same time as I fell into yours, and I feel like everything moved so fast, and yet it's not moving fast enough. So, yes, it's okay to be worried about me. It's okay to be relieved that it wasn't me lying in that chair today. Because I'm thankful, too. Yet I'm broken up like jagged shards of memory and pain because a man that I called my friend, a man who was truly a better person than I could ever hope to be is gone."

They were both crying then, and Tessa didn't know what to do so she wrapped her arms around him and just held him close.

"I love you," she whispered, the words forced out of her in a rush. She hadn't meant to tell him that, not yet, maybe not for a long while. She had wanted to make sure those words were true, wanted to make sure she wasn't just over-feeling things. But she loved this man. "I love you so damn much, Murphy Gallagher, and I can't lose you."

"Jesus Christ, Tessa. I love you so damn much, too. I've been trying to think about how to tell you all day, and then everything went to shit, and I was afraid if I told you now, you'd think it was because of what happened. But damn it, baby, I love you. I love you so much. I never thought I'd feel this way, and I tried my best not to fall for you because you're my best friend."

"And your roommate," she teased, her body shaking. The ups and downs of the day were taking their toll on her, so she just held onto Murphy, doing her best not to hyper-ventilate with all she was feeling.

He smiled down at her, tears mixed with sheer happiness in his eyes. "And your roommate." He leaned down and kissed her, and she melted into him, needing him closer and never wanting to let go.

This isn't who I was before, she thought. She'd never thought she would crave a man as much as she did Murphy. She needed him in her body and soul. Yet it felt as though it had been the right thing all along because she wasn't merely giving herself to him, he was giving himself to her in return.

This wasn't like before, this wasn't like her controlling ex or Brent or any of the men she'd casually dated in the past.

This was *Murphy*.

And he was everything.

He ran his hand through her hair and hugged her tightly. "I...I need you," he whispered. "I need to hold you, to be with you. I need to remember this day not for what was taken, but for what can come from us. Are you up for that?" He kissed her again, his touch tentative, sweet. "Tell me what you're thinking?"

She went up on her tiptoes in answer and kissed him again. "I need you, too. I need to remember what it feels like to have you in my arms and inside me. I need...I just *need*."

And with that, he tugged her back to her bedroom and slowly stripped her out of her clothes as she did the same to him. There were no words needed as they kissed and touched. There would be time for words later, time for grief over what was lost. For now, they only had each other, and their touches and caresses were proof of that.

When she wrapped her hand around his already hard cock, he let out a groan and pulled away. "I'm sensitive," he whispered against her mouth before sliding his fingers between her legs. "I won't last long with your hands on me."

She sucked on his tongue before pulling back. "You had treatment today, Murphy. Let me take care of you." Gently, she pushed him back onto her bed so he lay with his head on the pillows and his body spread before her. After quickly getting out the massage oil and condoms and a hand towel from the nightstand, she went to straddle his waist, careful not to put her body weight on him and end up hurting him.

"Let me love you," she whispered.

His hands went to her waist. "As long as you let me love you."

She swallowed hard. "Always." And she prayed that *always* would be far longer than a mere breath. After squirting some of the oil on her hands, she rubbed her palms together to warm it up, then began massaging his chest and arms. Murphy gathered up some of the oil as well and rubbed her arms and chest too, playing with her nipples and breasts just enough that she had to squirm where she sat.

Soon, they were both panting, and they'd only innocently touched one another, so she wiped her hands on the towel and opened the condom before sliding it down over his length. Then, keeping her eyes on his, she slowly lowered herself on top of him. They both moaned, their bodies slick, wet, and ready.

"I love you," he whispered, his voice tight. "I didn't expect to fall in love with you, but you're my best surprise."

She rolled her hips, her eyes rolling to the back of her head as she did so. "You're my favorite surprise," she said softly. "I love you, too."

They made love slowly as if they were afraid if they went too fast, it would all be over soon and out of their grasp. And when they came, they did so together, collapsing in a pile, holding onto one another as if they couldn't let go.

She rested her head on his oiled and sweat-slick chest, knowing they both needed a shower, but not caring. She needed to hear his heartbeat, needed to feel it beneath her cheek.

A man had died today, and yet it wasn't Murphy. The fact that it could have been sent a chill sweeping over her. The man she loved held her close, and she knew her thoughts weren't that much different than his.

Time was never on their side, but maybe, just maybe, Tessa could believe in hope. Because without hope, she wasn't sure she could go on.

18

"Tessa, can I see you in my office for a moment?"

Tessa turned at the sound of her boss's voice and nodded, praying the exhaustion she felt deep down in her bones didn't show on her face. She hadn't been sleeping too well since Max had lost his fight right in front of her, and she'd bared her soul to Murphy. She kept waking up in a sweat thanks to nightmares where it was Murphy who gave her a wide-eyed look before leaving her forever. What made it worse was that Murphy was having similar dreams and waking up right along with her. They would either hold each other until one of them finally fell asleep, or make love until they were both too exhausted to dream. Now, she felt like a walking zombie, and she knew Murphy had to be feeling the same.

His brothers weren't letting him on the jobsites other than to walk around the side of them and check in. They knew as well as she did that though Murphy might be finished with this first round of treatment, they still weren't out of the woods.

Although she and Murphy had declared their love for one another, things still felt as if they could fall away from her at any moment. They had gone to the funeral together yesterday to say goodbye to one of Murphy's first friends. She'd almost broken down when she witnessed Abby's strength at the gravesite. The other woman had said her goodbyes; her cheeks dry from tears, but she'd looked broken beyond measure. Even so, Tessa knew that Abby would put all her energy into her unborn child. And no matter what, Tessa would make sure she was there for her. She had a feeling that Murphy would help her, but Tessa would be there for Abby, as well.

But Tessa wasn't at the gravesite today and had to remember where she was.

"Of course," she said, reminding herself that she was at work and needed to focus and not have her head in memories and promises. She followed her boss to his office, giving her coworkers nods as she passed.

Gerald Randleman had been working at the hospital for longer than she could remember, and was a decent boss. He was scarce on the compliments but never belittled anyone in public. In fact, he usually brought someone back to his office to reprimand them now that she thought about it, and suddenly, she wished she hadn't had that third cup of coffee.

"Take a seat, Tessa," he said as he gestured toward the chair opposite his side of the desk. He sat down before she did so she quickly scurried to take a seat, as well.

"What can I do for you, Gerald?" she asked, keeping her tone light and professional.

He tapped a file on his desk, and she looked down to see her name on the tab. Oh, hell. She could *not* lose her job right now. Her best friend had been let go from this very hospital because of budget cuts, and though Liz now worked at a place better suited for her, Tessa didn't want to have to find a new job. She *liked* the hospital, even if she worked long hours.

"I've been doing performance reviews for everyone under my umbrella over the past few weeks. You know there were budget cuts recently, and now they're pushing us to do *another* cut."

Tessa bit her tongue so she wouldn't say something and get herself fired sooner. She was damn good at her job and did all she could for those in her care, but that could have been said of Liz also, and look what had happened to her.

"I brought you in here to tell you something I don't tell everyone," he continued as if she hadn't been going through worst-case scenarios in her mind the entire time. "You are an asset to this hospital."

She froze, her eyes going wide. "Excuse me?"

Her boss did something then that he rarely did, he smiled. "You heard me, you are an asset. You put a hundred and twenty percent of yourself into each case that you get.

These patients aren't just numbers and insurance codes to you. You want them to be healthy, but you also don't want them walking out of this building with impending debt and even more tears. Though you never cross the line. You never twist the rules to your benefit. But you spend hours making sure that you do every single thing you can for these people. You put your all into it, and I for one am grateful. And my bosses noticed, too. So keep doing what you're doing, and one day, you might just have my job or end up being my boss." He winked as he spoke, and Tessa just blinked.

This was totally not what she'd been expecting, and she wasn't sure she could fully process everything he had just said.

"Oh, well, thank you." She knew she sounded like an idiot, but she really hadn't been prepared for any of that.

Gerald nodded before sliding her file underneath a stack of others. "I just thought you should know. So keep up the good work and get back out there. Close the door on your way out, please."

Dismissed, Tessa did as he asked and went back out to her small desk. She couldn't quite believe everything that had been said in Gerald's office. But the truth was, she did put her all into her job. She didn't work as hard as she did for the accolades; she did it for the people she was trying to help. She put her all into her work and was now trying to find a balance between that and a life she could have with someone else.

But in order to do that, she knew she had to do something she should've done a long time ago. And, thankfully, she'd already made plans that could help her tonight. Maybe, just maybe, she could handle it all.

"ARE you sure you want me with you?" Murphy asked from the driver's seat. He gave her a look as he pulled into her parents' driveway. "I can just drop you off if you'd rather do this alone."

Tessa leaned forward and kissed his cheek, loving the soft beard he now wore since he wasn't shaving anymore thanks to his blood issues and not wanting to risk getting a slight cut that might get infected. He might be on the right track to bruising less and being able to shave again, but she loved his beard and didn't want him to get rid of it. It felt so good in...certain places.

"You've met my parents before—without me, I might add—so it's not like you're meeting them for the first time. Yes, this is sort of a get-to-know-the-parents thing, but they already love you like I do. Okay, maybe not exactly like I do, but you get the picture." She was rambling just a bit since she was nervous about tonight, but she'd get over it soon. However, she knew she needed Murphy there. He was her rock—something she hadn't expected to have—and now he was stuck with her.

Murphy turned off the engine and leaned forward, capturing her lips in an intoxicating kiss that made her wish they weren't sitting in her parents' driveway.

"You need me, I'm there," he said softly.

"I know." And she did. It was so weird relying on someone as she was. *Knowing* they would always be there. Before, she'd only thought Liz would fit that role, and yet she knew Murphy would always be there no matter what. It was daunting and warming all at the same time.

"Let's do this, then," he said with a wink. "I'll be your charming boyfriend and promise not to keep you out too late."

She smiled widely, loving the sparkle in his eyes. He hadn't had that intensity since Max's death, and she knew he was still hurting—they both were—but he was healing.

"You can keep me out as late as you want, Gallagher. I'll just be sure to find a nice little plaid skirt to wear when you do."

He groaned and adjusted himself before narrowing his eyes. "I'm *not* going into that house with a hard-on, so stop."

She winced, knowing they'd gone a little too far in their play, even though she liked that just her words could make him hard. "Think about Graham's bare ass. That'll help."

Murphy winced before letting out a chuckle. "Well, that's one way to do it. Let's go, baby." They both laughed and got out of the car and headed up the walkway to her parents' front door. They didn't even have to knock before Tessa's mom was opening the door and smiling widely.

"I saw you pull up, but your dad held me back from going out and meeting you at the car. I'm trying to be better about waiting for you to at least get to the door before I open it."

Her mom opened her arms, and Tessa walked right into them, hugging her back hard. Tears stung the backs of her eyes for some reason, and she inhaled that soft scent that was uniquely her mom and reminded her of the good things from her childhood.

"I'm so glad you're here, baby. Now go hug your dad so I can hug this very handsome young man you brought with you." Her mom winked, and Tessa laughed before going into her father's arms. Her dad squeezed her tightly, and out of the corner of her eye, Tessa saw Murphy hug her mom hard before handing over the flowers in his hand. Yeah, her man was a charmer all right, and that was just fine with her.

Murphy said hello to her father as her mom led Tessa into the kitchen where they put the flowers in a vase, and Tessa helped her mom set up for dinner. Murphy and her dad walked in soon after and helped set the table. Her mom had already done most of the work, so all Tessa really had to do was stir the potatoes before putting them in the serving dish. By the time they sat down, the table was laden with roast beef, creamy gravy, potatoes, two kinds of vegetables, and homemade rolls. Tessa's stomach growled, and she had a feeling someone would have to roll her out of the house after she finished eating.

"This looks fantastic," Murphy said after pulling out Tessa's chair. *Such a gentleman.*

"Thank you." Her mom beamed. "Since this is the first

time Tessa has brought a boy home in a long while, I wanted it to be special."

Tessa held back a wince at the reminder of her ex, but her parents moved on to the subject of Murphy's family business. Her parents only knew some of the story when it came to Andy, and she wasn't sure if she would ever tell them everything. There was no use worrying them over something that couldn't be changed. But once dinner was over, she did have a few things to say.

They gorged themselves on the best roast beef she had ever had, and she was pretty sure she ate about a dozen rolls, but she didn't care. She'd just go on that evil run tomorrow so she could fit into her bridesmaid's dress for Liz, and not regret a single thing she inhaled tonight.

They cleaned up as a group, Murphy doing the dishes so her mom didn't have to. From that move alone, Tessa knew Murphy had endeared himself to her parents. And though he was truly being a nice guy and probably sucking up to her mom and dad, she had a feeling he would've done the dishes anyway. The Gallaghers had been raised right.

After dinner, Tessa's stomach rolled, and at that point, she regretted how much she'd eaten. Murphy knew what she planned to say tonight, and she had even practiced it a few times with him. She just hoped she didn't make a fool of herself.

"Mom? Dad? Do you have a moment? I have a few things I'd like to say."

Dad gave her a weird look, and her mom looked

worried. She hated that concerned look, it was something she had seen all too often. That was part of the reason why she was here tonight.

"What is it, darling? You know you can talk to us about anything." Her mom patted the seat beside her on the couch, but Tessa shook her head.

"I think I need to stand for this, if that's okay." She took a deep breath and figured she needed to start from the beginning. "I know I wasn't the best kid."

"Now, Tessa, don't say that," her dad began, but she held up her hand to stop him.

"Let me just say what I need to, okay? I needed to say something like this long ago." She looked over at Murphy, and he gave her a nod. She rolled her shoulders back, grateful that he was there for her.

"I wasn't the best kid," she repeated, "but I had the best parents. I don't know why I kept pushing you guys away, but I think it maybe had to do with me thinking I had to make you guys prove that you would never leave me. When I look back on it, all I see are stupid decisions and fear that I would end up alone. You guys loved me from day one. You saved me. And I threw it back in your faces. I think I did it because I knew you guys wouldn't leave. You guys would never stop loving me even when I didn't love myself. So I just want to say thank you for being the parents that I needed, the parents that I wanted, and the parents that, at some point, I didn't think I deserved."

"Oh, baby," her mother cried, but didn't move to get up,

and for that, Tessa was grateful because she wasn't sure she could continue if she had.

"I put you guys through hell because I had this notion that I needed to find myself. I was stupid, and I made poor decisions that hurt everybody around me, especially you. You got hurt because I was an idiot who couldn't listen to authority."

"You changed," her dad said firmly. "You learned from your mistakes."

Tessa nodded. "You're right. I did. But I never apologized for those mistakes. And because of that, I ended up pushing you guys away when I shouldn't have. I was the one who put this distance between us, and for that, I am sorry. I never want that distance again. I never want you guys to feel like you have to be on the outside, looking into my life. I want you to be part of my future and my present. I love you guys so much, and I want you to be a part of my life, I want to be part of your lives, more than just a dinner when we can arrange it. So, if you can forgive me for putting up those walls, I would love to be able to tear them down with you."

Tessa's mom was openly crying, and her dad had tears in his eyes, as well. Before she knew it, they were both standing and opening their arms for her as she rushed toward them, hugging them tightly.

"You're our daughter," her dad said, his voice stern. "You were from day one. I don't care what blood says, you're *ours*. And you didn't have to apologize for what you did as a child and teen. You more than proved yourself as a young woman.

But the fact that you did tells me we raised you right. You're such a good person, Tessa. We love you."

"And, yes, we want to be part of your life even more," her mom said with a little cry. "You're our baby girl. But I have to warn you, now that you've let me in, I'm hard to get out." She looked over Tessa's shoulder. "That means you, too, young man. If you're part of our baby girl's life, then I'm going to want to mother you just as much."

Tessa pulled away slightly so she could look at Murphy. He'd stood and had a giant grin on his face.

"I think I can do that. In fact, I think you and my mom would have gotten along just fine."

That set Tessa's mom off again, and Murphy somehow ended up in their giant hug, laughing with them as Tessa's heart healed even more. She should have let go of her pain and guilt long ago, but she'd been scared. Now, though, she could feel the weight being lifted off her chest and knew that from this day forward, things would be different.

She wasn't the same Tessa Stone she used to be: scared of where she'd come from and on edge because of it. She'd made poor choices and had run into the arms of the wrong man before, but that wasn't now.

Now, she had Murphy, her family, a job that valued her, and a life she could see coming together one day at a time.

Finally.

By the time they made it home, Tessa was exhausted and

exhilarated at the same time. She was stuffed from dessert, and her heart was full to the brim.

"I'm proud of you," Murphy said as he pulled in next to her car. "I know you were scared, but you rocked it. And your parents are pretty amazing."

She beamed at him, leaning back in her seat. "They are. And now they'll be stopping by to see the house." She winced. "So I guess we should probably actually clean up a bit." She paused. "And maybe just move you into my room and make the other room an office or something." She didn't look at him as she said the last part, her words spilling out of her mouth quickly.

Murphy kissed her hand. "I think I'm going to like waking up to you every morning. Now let's get you inside so I can rub your feet."

Her toes curled since she knew he wouldn't only be rubbing her feet by the end of the night. She got out of the truck as quickly as she could since she wasn't all that tall and there was nothing graceful about sliding out of the darn thing, and made her way to the porch, only to freeze.

"What..."

"Why is the porch light out?" Murphy asked as he walked to her side. "I thought we turned it on before we left."

Tessa tried to speak but came up empty. "There's something on the porch." Her words were a whisper.

Murphy tugged her behind him and cursed. "That's a damn dead bird." He paused. "A *big* dead bird. Looks like a goose. And it's fucking torn open like a wild animal got to it."

Chills slid up Tessa's back, and she gripped Murphy's shirt. "I think we need to call the police."

He frowned down at her. "What?"

"Between this and the tires...I don't know...something feels off." She looked around, feeling as if someone were watching her. In fact, every instance where she'd felt *off* in the past few weeks came back to her, and bile filled her throat. "I think someone's watching us."

Murphy cursed again and tugged her toward Owen and Liz's. "We're going to call the cops from my brother's. And you're going to tell me anything that's happened lately that seemed weird, even if it's nothing. Because you're right, that bird didn't just die on our porch."

She pressed her lips together, fear coating her tongue. There was something going on, and she was missing a key element, she just didn't know what it was. But she had this sudden fear that if she didn't figure it out soon, it would be too late.

19

It had been two days since the cops had left her house after asking her questions, and they weren't any closer to figuring things out than they had been before she called them. In fact, the more they asked her to provide details, the more she thought maybe she'd just imagined everything.

A large cat could have left the dead bird on her porch; they *were* in Colorado by the mountains, after all.

Kids could have slashed Murphy's tires because they thought it would be fun.

No one was in her car the morning she'd felt that things had been moved around. She'd just been overtired and in need of more coffee.

And having the hairs on the back of her neck stand on end could have just been a chill or a temperature change, not the sudden awareness that someone was watching her.

Yes, the list of all those things might make it sound like

things were escalating, but there was no way to tie them all together, so Tessa figured she had imagined everything. The police had taken her statement, but she could tell that they weren't sure this was an actual incident either.

Murphy, on the other hand, was livid. Not that she hadn't mentioned some of those things, but because they were happening at all.

And she was pretty sure that if today hadn't been Owen and Liz's wedding day in their backyard, Murphy would still be grumbling and far too overprotective. However, *because* it was her best friend and practically sister's wedding day, Tessa was going to push all those thoughts from her mind and focus on the only thing that mattered.

Liz and Owen's big day.

"I can't believe how quickly everything came together," Blake said from her seat in Liz's bedroom. The women had decided to take over Liz's house while the men were at Tessa and Murphy's so the bride and groom wouldn't see each other. It might be a backyard wedding, but they had gone all out to make sure it was the perfect event for these two.

"This is Liz and Owen we're talking about, *of course,* it came together as fast as it did." Maya stood by the window looking out into the backyard where the seats and wedding venue had been set up.

Tessa couldn't help but grin at that since her backyard had also been taken over in the process. It was a good thing they hadn't put the fence back up between the two properties since it made it easier for them to spread out and make a backyard wedding look like a fairy princess's dream.

As it was, flower girl Rowan was already bouncing in her lacy, pale peach dress. "It's *so* pretty." Rowan picked at one of her curls, and Blake reached out and tugged at her daughter's hand. Once the wedding was over, Tessa was pretty sure that the little girl's shoes would be off and her hair undone, but she didn't figure Blake would care. As long as they made it through the ceremony with shoes on, it was a win.

Liz smiled at them from her side of the room where she stood with Tessa in front of a full-length mirror they'd brought in for the occasion. "We wanted tiny lights for when it got darker and light-colored flowers. Nothing too ostentatious, but perfectly simple for Owen and me."

"You guys nailed it," Tessa said softly and kissed her friend's temple. "And I have to say, this dress is *stunning*."

Liz blushed and ran her hand over her baby bump. "We wanted something that would work if I started to show more...and since I popped out last week, I'm glad we did." Tessa had gone with Liz to pick out the floor-length white dress that had a lace overlay and a waist that billowed out just enough to cover her baby bump at any size. Her best friend looked like a Grecian goddess, and Tessa knew she wouldn't make it through the day without crying. Thank God for waterproof makeup.

"You did good," Tessa said with a smile. "And I think your bridesmaids look pretty kickass.

Maya, Blake, and Tessa had gone with variations of the peach color, and each wore a different dress to highlight their figures. Everything was light and airy and perfect for an outdoor, summer wedding that was still casual.

"Wait, are you guys bridesmaids if you're married? I know the maid of honor is really the matron of honor if she's married, but what about the others?" Tessa was the maid of honor, while Graham was the best man. She knew Liz had thought about pairing up couples, but everyone had decided it would be much more fun to switch it up. That left Tessa with Graham, Blake with Jake, Maya with Murphy, and Border would be walking Noah down the aisle next to Rowan as the supervising ring bearer. Considering everyone would just end up with their significant others once the ceremony was over, it didn't really matter who walked whom down the aisle. They were all one big giant family anyway.

The entire Montgomery clan would also be showing up, as well as some of Liz's former and current coworkers. The couple had also invited Abby, but the other woman had declined to no one's surprise. Once the wedding was over, however, Tessa planned to spend more time with Abby. The other woman didn't have that much family, and Tessa and Murphy didn't want the woman to ever feel like she was alone.

"Are you ready to become a Gallagher?" Blake asked. "I mean, once you're in, they kind of don't let you go."

Liz's smile was so bright that Tessa finally let a tear fall down her cheek. "I feel like I've been waiting my whole life to be a Gallagher. Not only is the man I love one, some of my favorite people are, as well." She gave Tessa a wry look. "And a certain best friend of mine might just end up being a Gallagher in the end also."

If Rowan hadn't been there, Tessa would have flipped her best friend off. As it was, she glared at Liz before rolling her eyes. She and Murphy might be serious, and they might be living together beyond just being roommates, but she wanted some time before she took that next step. Falling in love had been scary enough that she wanted to soak in that feeling for a bit. Talk of marriage and everything that came with that could wait just a little while longer.

The ladies helped Liz finish getting ready until the time came, and soon they were outside waiting to walk down the aisle so Liz and Owen could finally become husband and wife.

"You look fucking amazing," Murphy whispered in her ear, his hands around her waist, giving her a squeeze. "I can't wait to ruck that skirt up to your hips and fuck you so hard your breasts bounce right out of that top. Seriously, what was Liz thinking, dressing you up like a peach? It just makes me want to take a bite, and lick and...suck."

She knew her cheeks were bright red, but she ignored him, considering her parents were sitting right in front of them with the rest of their friends and family. Murphy Gallagher was a very bad boy, and she really, *really* liked it.

Before she could say anything, Graham tugged her away

and into his side. "Keep your hands off my date." He waggled his eyebrows as he said it, and Blake threw her head back and laughed.

"That's my husband over there, Tessa Stone. Be gentle," the other woman teased.

They were still far enough back that though they could see the audience, no one could hear them except for the wedding party. Owen stood by the officiant, and Border had the kids off to the side, so Tessa didn't mind whispering what she was about to say.

"I'll keep my hands off your husband, but don't I remember hearing a story about you having your hands all over my boyfriend's dick?"

Murphy let out a choked laugh, and Graham pinched the bridge of his nose. "Dear God, Tessa."

"What? It's true. Isn't it? Didn't Blake pierce that very pretty dick of yours?"

Blake nudged her in the side and laughed. "You know, it really was a pretty dick. You're one very lucky woman."

Tessa grinned. "Yes, I am. And thank you for the piercing, I love it."

Jake, Murphy, and Graham each let out a groan. Maya, Blake, and Tessa just gave each other high fives and grinned.

"I can't believe I'm going to have Murphy's dick on my mind when I walk down the aisle," Liz said wryly.

"Just think about your soon-to-be husband's, and you'll

be fine." Maya patted Liz gently on the shoulder, though there was laughter in her eyes.

"I have no idea how I became part of this family, but I am so happy that I get to go up with all of you and tell the man I love that I'm going to be with him forever. Thank you so much for being with me today. For being with *us* today. You have no idea how much this means to both of us. Now, come on, because I do not want to wait any longer to call Owen mine and become Mrs. Liz Gallagher."

And with that, everyone took his or her places as the music started up. Tessa glanced at Murphy one last time and smiled, knowing that today was only the beginning. Tomorrow would be even better.

THE PARTY WAS in full swing, the newly married couple softly kissed one another as they swayed in the center of the homemade dancing area. Sometimes it paid to have people in the family who knew how to use their hands and could build pretty much anything.

Tessa leaned into Murphy's hold, swaying gently to the music. She knew he didn't have as much energy as he wanted to go out there and dance the night away, but it didn't matter to her. She had the arms of the man she loved wrapped around her, and all she wanted to do was stay there.

Unfortunately, she'd had too much punch and really

needed to use the restroom. Though Tessa had offered to open up her house for the wedding, Liz and Owen had nixed that idea, saying that their house would be more than enough for everyone since it had three bathrooms, and they didn't want everyone taking over Tessa's home. That meant that her bathrooms would be free, and she wouldn't need to wait in line.

Thank God.

"I'll be right back, I have to go to the little maid of honor's room." She turned in Murphy's arms and kissed him softly. "Love you."

His eyes darkened. "Love you, too, Tessa mine." She kissed him again and made her way toward her house, smiling at those she passed. Everyone seemed to be having such a wonderful time, and she was glad that Liz and Owen had decided to have the wedding where they had.

She unlocked her back door and walked inside, turning on the hall light to guide her way since the sun was just now setting. She went into her master bath, did her business, and checked her makeup since there were still a few photos being taken. Smiling, she adjusted her dress and couldn't help but blush at the thought of what Murphy would do to it—and her—later.

She was just about to head through the back door when she heard a noise coming from the kitchen. Murphy must have come inside to grab something. With a smile on her face, she walked toward the kitchen and froze.

"Andy? What are you doing in here?" Fear crackled up her spine and settled in her belly. Though every instinct told her to run, she knew it would be a mistake. She stood in place, not quite comprehending what was happening.

Her ex-boyfriend ran his hand over his neatly pressed suit and shook his head at her, frowning. "Why wouldn't I be here, Tessa? Why do you think you can run from me?"

She blinked, confused yet still scared of what might happen. She hadn't heard from Andy in years, and yet it sounded as if he had been thinking about her all this time.

"I don't know what you mean. You should go, Andy."

Her mind felt as if she were a half step behind what was going on, until everything finally clicked. The bird, the tires, the car, the feeling of being watched...seeing him earlier in town. Everything finally made sense, and yet the nausea sliding its way through her made her want to flee and forget that any of that had happened.

"I'm not leaving anytime soon, Tessa. And you do not get to leave either. You don't get to leave me. Not again. I got rid of the damn pencil pusher. That asshole Brent. I can't believe you'd be with some little prick that ran away as quickly as he did, but he left when I told him to. But then Murphy got in the way. Murphy always gets in the way." He took a deep breath, and Tessa tried to inch toward the doorway behind her, only to stop when he shot her a dangerous look. "Don't move. Don't you fucking move. I thought you'd finally pay attention and look at me when I left you that present on your doorstep, but you didn't even see me. You didn't see me when I slashed that asshole's tires. You didn't see me when I walked through your office and got the keys to your car. You never saw me. And that was your first mistake. Or maybe your first mistake was calling the cops on me in the first place all those years ago. You are mine, Tessa. You don't get to just walk away because you think you're tired of me. You're the one who made the error, and now, you're the one who's going to pay."

"You should go," she whispered. "Please, Andy, please just let me go."

Oh God. What was happening? How could *any* of this be happening? He'd done all of that to her. He'd either threatened Brent or had told her ex so many lies that he'd walked away without a second glance. Andy had stalked her, and knew far too many things; things that she'd never dreamed possible.

And now he wasn't going to let her go.

How...how was she going to get out of this?

Only, she wasn't sure she was going to be able to get out of this at all.

"The only place you're going is with me. You're going to forget about that fucker outside and be mine until I decide I'm done with you. And that's not going to be anytime soon."

Then he moved.

It wasn't until she saw the light glinting off the metal that she noticed the largest butcher knife she had was missing from the block. He came at her, knife raised, and she ducked. She shouldered him in the stomach, and he let out an *oof*. After she'd kicked him in the shin, she ran towards the front door, knowing she needed to get out of the house.

But he pulled on her hair, tugging it from its arrangement and forcing her backwards. She turned and put her hand up to cover her face from the oncoming blade. She screamed as the knife plunged into her forearm and sliced down.

Scorching pain radiated and shocked her system, causing bile to crawl up her throat. She kicked out and clamped her hand over the gushing wound on her arm, falling back on her butt at the movement. Andy screamed and looked down at the blood covering the blade.

Tessa scooted back so she pressed along the wall, holding her arm against her. The fact that the cut didn't hurt any more than it did told her that it was much worse than she'd thought.

"Tessa?"

Murphy's voice filtered into her ears, and tears spilled down her cheeks.

Andy turned at the sound of her lover's voice, and she was afraid that Murphy was too late.

She was too late.

20

M urphy took in the scene and tried to figure out exactly what he was seeing. Tessa sat on the floor at the other end of the kitchen, holding her bloody arm to her chest. Red stained the tile and the peach of her dress, and her face had gone far too pale.

"You should have stayed outside, Murphy," a cruel voice whispered, the tone ice-cold.

Murphy looked up into his friend Hugh's eyes and tried to keep his erratic heartbeat under control. He didn't know what the fuck was going on, but whatever he was seeing in front of him had to be a dream.

There was no way this was happening.

"Hugh? What...?"

"Hugh?" Tessa gasped.

His childhood friend smiled, but there was nothing good in that expression, nothing innocent. "You caught me.

Fate has a hell of a good time when it comes to putting us together, I think. My name is Hugh Anderson Greenwood, but everyone called me Andy in college. Anderson's a family name and before *you*, I was able to use it to my advantage. I dropped the name Hugh for a while, enjoying being a new person, but when Tessa over here set the cops on me, I went back to Hugh. Who would have thought my woman, the one who shouldn't have run from me, would end up in your arms, Murphy? You shouldn't have touched her. She's *mine*."

Murphy's brain tried to keep up, but he felt like he was missing so many things. He put all of that out of his mind, though, all the whys and what-ifs and focused on the bloody knife in Hugh's hand, as well as the fact that Tessa was looking paler by the minute.

Murphy had to get to her, had to find someone to help her, but he had to get through to Hugh—*Andy*—first. Bile coated his tongue, and his mind went through dozens of scenarios as he tried to figure out how to get to Tessa and not end up hurting her or himself in the process. Only Murphy was unarmed, and Hugh was unbalanced.

"You never should have slept with her. You never should have been her roommate. I finally found her after all this time, and she was with you? You're just a poor excuse for a man who needs drugs to stay alive. The cancer should've taken you when you were a kid, that way, I wouldn't even have to look at you and your helpless little face. You don't deserve her. She's mine."

Then Hugh lunged. Murphy ducked out of the way,

missing the edge of the knife by mere inches. If he got cut, even just a little, he could bleed out. His blood was far too thin thanks to the cancer and chemo, and he didn't clot the way he should. But right then, he didn't care. The only thing that mattered was Tessa.

Hugh swiped out again, this time leaning forward as he did. Protecting his face, Murphy grabbed the other man's wrist and pushed. Hugh attacked again, and then somehow, they were falling. Murphy landed on his back, his head smashing into the tile floor, and Hugh landed on top of him. The breath was knocked out of Murphy, and his head ached something fierce, but he wasn't sure where the knife had gone. Everything had moved so fast, and the adrenaline pumped through his system so quickly he didn't even know if he was hurt.

Blood pooled around them, and Murphy heard Tessa scream.

And yet, neither Hugh nor Murphy moved.

It was over.

Forever.

"Are you sure the doctor said you were okay?" Liz asked, cupping Murphy's face. She still wore her wedding gown with Owen's jacket over her shoulders.

"I'm fine," he mumbled, not feeling fine but not physically hurt either.

Tessa's scream had been loud enough that others had

come running into the house right after Murphy had fallen. They'd kept the children away, but the rest of his family had shown up to see what had happened.

Liz's dress still had streaks of blood on it from taking care of Tessa. She'd been the only one with medical training in attendance and hadn't thought twice about ruining her dress.

Everything had happened quickly after that with the police and emergency crew filling the house within ten minutes. They had whisked Tessa off in an ambulance along with her mother since Murphy had needed to be checked out on his own and there hadn't been any time for any other decisions.

Once the paramedics had assured Murphy that he wasn't in danger of a concussion, they'd sent him to the emergency room anyway because of his history.

Hugh had been pronounced dead at the scene.

It seemed that when they'd hit the ground, Hugh had somehow fallen on his own knife. It had hit him right in the side, probably slicing through his liver. He'd died quickly. Murphy's hand had still been on Hugh's wrist when the police had arrived, but after a quick statement and one look at the scene, they'd known it was self-defense.

All of that, however, had happened in a fog. Murphy could only think of Tessa and the fact that she was in surgery. The knife had gone deep into her forearm, and they needed to ensure that there would be minimal nerve damage. She'd have to go through physical therapy and would probably end up with some loss of function in her arm and hand, but she was alive.

Hugh, or Andy, or whatever the fuck the psycho had called himself, could have hurt her worse.

And Murphy wouldn't have been able to stop it.

"How could I not have seen it?" he mumbled to himself, but the others in the waiting room didn't hear. Though Maya and Border were back at their house with Rowan and Noah, the rest of his family, and Tessa's parents were in the waiting room with him. Everyone was still in his or her wedding gear, but it all looked rumpled, bloody—like the scene of a crime.

"You weren't with him long," Jake said softly. "You hadn't seen him in years, and when you meet up with a childhood friend, no one goes into it thinking that they're meeting up with a stalker or killer. It's not your fault, Murphy."

"He went by another name. There was no way that you'd think he was the same guy who had been with Tessa in the past. And didn't you say that she never actually told you her ex's name?" Graham added.

"I knew Hugh was a different man than he was back in the day, but I thought it was because we'd grown up, grown apart, and liked different things." Murphy rubbed his face, exhausted but needing to see Tessa. "There was so much blood..." He swallowed hard. "What if she lost too much?"

Liz sank into the chair next to him, resting her hand on her belly. "She *did* lose a lot of blood, but she has some of the best surgeons in the state working on her right now. I know these people, and Tessa does, too. They're going to make sure she gets the best care available. She should be out of surgery soon, and then you can go visit her." She gestured toward Grace and Chris. "Along with her parents."

Grace held her husband's hand, though neither of them had cried. It was as if they were in shock, but there was also a determination in their gazes as if they were willing their baby girl to be okay.

Murphy stood up then and passed his family to kneel in front of the Stones. "I'm sorry I didn't get there sooner."

Grace shook her head and cupped his face while Chris gripped his shoulder. "You saved our baby girl. I don't even want to think about what might have happened if you hadn't shown up when you did."

Chris let out a huffed breath. "And I know that one cut could have hurt you, son. I know you risked everything for her. So I'd better not hear you blame yourself anymore. Do you hear me? My girl is going to need you to be strong and whole when she comes out of this. Don't make her worry about you, too."

"Listen to them," Owen put in, his voice low. "She's not going to blame you, Murph. She loves you."

Murphy let out a breath. He wasn't sure if he would be able to fully forgive himself for not seeing Hugh for whom he was, but he'd try for Tessa. First, however, he needed to see her, needed to make sure she was truly okay.

He ended up sitting next to Grace and held her other hand while his family talked around them. He didn't know what he'd do without them and was thankful that he didn't have to find out anytime soon. The Gallaghers never gave up, never walked away. And for that, he would always be grateful.

And when the doctors came in to tell him that Tessa was out of surgery and resting, he buried his face in his hands and finally let the tears come.

The love of his life was alive, and she would be okay. Thank God.

I won't take this for granted, he told himself. He wouldn't take her health or his for granted again.

They were both alive, and that meant he would do everything in his power so they could *live*.

WHEN THEY FINALLY LET HIM back to see her, her arm was wrapped up past her elbow, and she looked pale in her hospital bed, but he'd never seen anyone look so beautiful. Before he'd even stepped fully into the room, she fluttered open her eyes and gave him a small smile.

"Murphy," she rasped.

He quickly went to her side and gently touched her free hand. "Tessa." He squeezed his eyes shut, overcome with everything that had happened and trying to keep calm.

"Love you," she said with a sappy smile. He knew she was on some good pain meds, and he was just grateful they'd let him come back to see her at all.

"Love you, too, baby." He shuddered out a breath. "I'm so damn sorry."

Her eyes filled but she blinked them back. "Thank you for saving me."

He shook his head. "I'll always be there for you, just like I know you'll be there for me. Always."

She sighed, her eyes closing, and he knew he should go and let her sleep. "Stay," she whispered. "Stay."

So he sat down on the chair next to her bed and gripped her hand, watching her sleep as she healed.

He'd known he loved Tessa Stone, but it wasn't until then that he realized the depth of that emotion.

Tessa Stone was his for now and forever, and he'd spend the rest of his days proving that.

No matter what.

AFTER

Murphy gripped Tessa's hips, pounding into her as she wrapped one arm around his neck, meeting him thrust for thrust. Her other arm still had her wrap on it, so he made sure he didn't touch it. She might be mostly healed, but he'd be damned if he hurt her at all.

Over the past few weeks, they'd learned to take special care when they made love, but their enthusiasm and vigor hadn't waned a bit.

Hence why they were fucking on the bathroom counter right next to the place where they'd seen each other naked, *felt* each other naked, for the first time. He hadn't been able to keep his hands off her, and there was nothing better in the morning after a shower than having Tessa squeeze his dick with her pussy.

Seriously.

Nothing. Better.

Tessa arched her back again, and since her nipples were *right there,* he sucked one into his mouth, biting down gently. Her legs tightened around his waist, and he knew she was on the verge of coming, so he increased his speed and let go of her hip with one hand to flick her clit with his thumb.

"Murphy!" Her whole body shuddered as she came around his cock, and he sped up again, sweat pouring down his back. When his balls tightened, he grunted, the release flowing through him as he came hard inside her, filling her up.

Sweating and panting, he leaned forward and cupped the back of her head so he could steal a hard kiss. "Good fucking morning."

She licked her lips, her eyes dark. "I think we need another shower since we didn't use a condom and now I'm all sticky."

"I like you sticky," he teased.

"Oh, yes, you'd rather me smear you all over my body so everyone knows I'm yours like some caveman."

He grinned widely. "Sometimes, I'm crude, what can I say?"

"Sometimes?" she said softly, fluttering her eyelashes.

He shrugged and pulled out of her slowly, handing over a washcloth as he did. "All the time. But, Tessa baby, do you see the scratch marks and welts all over my back and shoulders? I'm pretty sure you mark me up more than I do you."

She shrugged though he saw the blush on her cheeks. "What can I say? You make me lose my mind."

He kissed her then, needing her taste. "That's what I like to hear."

"And now we're going to be late, you know, because we do need another shower. I can't go over to Liz and Owen's covered in your man juice."

Murphy threw his head back and laughed. "Man juice?"

Tessa winked and then swayed her hips on the way to the shower. His dick stood at attention once again, watching her ass move from side to side. He figured they were going to be even later for the family BBQ that afternoon.

Oh well, it wasn't as if it was the first time.

Tessa let out a sharp giggle when he followed her, pressing her to the tile, and Murphy fell that much more in love. Damn, he loved this woman and everything she made him feel.

He wouldn't trade it for anything.

OWEN GAVE Murphy a knowing look as he and Tessa walked over to his brother's house a good forty minutes late. Considering the flushed look on each of the women's faces in the room, however, Murphy figured he and Tessa hadn't been the only ones taking advantage of a lazy morning.

Blake and Liz were both nearing their due dates and were comparing pregnancy cravings, and Murphy just had to smile. He couldn't wait for more Gallaghers to be brought into the world, and honestly, he couldn't wait for one—or four—of his own.

Once he and Tessa were married next spring, the two of them were going to start trying for children. Since he'd gone through so much chemo in his life, though, they knew it might not happen, so they were also looking into adoption. Knowing them, they'd probably end up doing both, and that would be just fine with him. He couldn't wait to see Tessa as a mother, and knew that her parents were aching to be grandparents.

Maya, Jake, and Border were huddled on the love seat, grinning at one another as their son Noah played with Rowan on the floor in front of them. He'd never thought Jake would find his happily ever after with not one, but two people, but he knew that they'd found the perfect people for each other even if it seemed unconventional to some.

Graham sat next to Blake and fed her from his plate, his attention and care to her funny and heartwarming to see. Murphy knew his brother had gone through hell twice over in his life, and having Blake pregnant with his child had to be a lot on him, but he couldn't wait to see Graham with an infant in his arms once again. He was already a fantastic dad to Rowan, and Murphy knew Graham only got better with age—like most of the Gallaghers.

Owen came back into the house from the back deck where he'd been setting up the grill for the rest of the meal, and Murphy had to hold back a smile. His brother had clearly been running his hands through his hair over and over again as he went through all his mental lists. Murphy had a feeling Owen would have to loosen up a bit as a dad, and Liz would help him along. After all, no amount of lists could ever prepare you for fatherhood—at least Murphy assumed.

Tessa leaned into him then, and he wrapped his arm around her shoulders. "What are you thinking about over here?" she asked, her voice low.

Murphy kissed her forehead and sighed. "Just how much our family has changed over the past few years." He looked around at each brother once more and smiled. "We're better off with all of you. I mean, we were doing okay before, but with you guys? You made us better men."

Her eyes brightened, and she kissed his jaw. "I do love the Gallagher brothers. Y'all were sexy before, but now with children and wedding bands on your fingers? Oh, boy."

He narrowed his eyes. "I hope you only mean one Gallagher in particular."

The love of his life laughed, and he melted at the sound. She'd been laughing more and more since the accident, and was now finally back to her old self, though he even loved quiet Tessa. He loved all of her moods.

"You're my favorite Gallagher, Murphy. I promise."

"Damn straight, I am. And I can't wait for you to be a Gallagher, too." He brought up her ring finger with her engagement ring and kissed the sapphire they'd gone with instead of a diamond. "Love you, Tessa."

"Love you, too, Murph."

He held her close and laughed at something Jake said, sinking into the couch and knowing that today was one of those perfect days he would never forget. Nothing particularly amazing had happened, and yet it was perfect.

He had his family, his woman, and his future.

And after everything he'd lost and feared he could never have, he knew that he'd found the one thing he'd been missing all along.

Hope.

A NOTE FROM CARRIE ANN

Thank you so much for reading **HOPE RESTORED**. I do hope if you liked this story, that you would please leave a review! Reviews help authors *and* readers.

The Gallagher Brothers series is now complete and though I'm sad to say goodbye to the Gallaghers, they might make an appearance in the rest of the Montgomery Ink world with the Montgomery Ink, Whiskey and Lies, and Montgomery Ink: Colorado Springs series!

Don't miss out on the Montgomery Ink World!

- Montgomery Ink (The Denver Montgomerys)
- Montgomery Ink: Colorado Springs (The Colorado Springs Montgomery Cousins)
- Montgomery Ink: Boulder (The Boulder Montgomery Cousins)

- Gallagher Brothers (Jake's Brothers from Ink Enduring)
- Whiskey and Lies (Tabby's Brothers from Ink Exposed)
- Fractured Connections (Mace's sisters from Fallen Ink)
- Less Than (Dimitri's siblings from Restless Ink)

If you want to make sure you know what's coming next from me, you can sign up for my newsletter at www.CarrieAnnRyan.com; follow me on twitter at @CarrieAnnRyan, or like my Facebook page. I also have a Facebook Fan Club where we have trivia, chats, and other goodies. You guys are the reason I get to do what I do and I thank you.

Make sure you're signed up for my MAILING LIST so you can know when the next releases are available as well as find giveaways and FREE READS.

Happy Reading!

The Gallagher Brothers Series:
Book 1: Love Restored
Book 2: Passion Restored
Book 3: Hope Restored

Want to keep up to date with the next Carrie Ann Ryan Release? Receive Text Alerts easily!
Text CARRIE to 24587

ABOUT CARRIE ANN

Carrie Ann Ryan is the New York Times and USA Today bestselling author of contemporary and paranormal romance. Her works include the Montgomery Ink,

Redwood Pack, Talon Pack, and Gallagher Brothers series, which have sold over 2.0 million books worldwide. She started writing while in graduate school for her advanced degree in chemistry and hasn't stopped since. Carrie Ann has written over fifty novels and novellas with more in the works. When she's not writing about bearded tattooed men or alpha wolves that need to find their mates, she's reading as much as she can and exploring the world of baking and gourmet cooking.

www.CarrieAnnRyan.com

MORE FROM CARRIE ANN

Montgomery Ink: Colorado Springs

The Fractured Connections Series:
A Montgomery Ink Spin Off Series

The Montgomery Ink: Boulder Series:

The Less Than Series:

A Montgomery Ink Spin Off Series

Book 1: Breathless With Her

Book 2: Reckless With You

The Elements of Five Series:

Book 1: From Breath and Ruin

Book 2: From Flame and Ash

Montgomery Ink:

Book 0.5: Ink Inspired

Book 0.6: Ink Reunited

Book 1: Delicate Ink

Book 1.5: Forever Ink

Book 2: Tempting Boundaries

Book 3: Harder than Words

Book 4: Written in Ink

Book 4.5: Hidden Ink

Book 5: Ink Enduring

Book 6: Ink Exposed

Book 6.5: Adoring Ink

Book 6.6: Love, Honor, & Ink

Book 7: Inked Expressions

Book 7.3: Dropout

Book 7.5: Executive Ink

Book 8: Inked Memories

Book 8.5: Inked Nights

Book 8.7: Second Chance Ink

The Gallagher Brothers Series:

A Montgomery Ink Spin Off Series

Book 1: Love Restored

Book 2: Passion Restored

Book 3: Hope Restored

The Whiskey and Lies Series:

A Montgomery Ink Spin Off Series

Book 1: Whiskey Secrets

Book 2: Whiskey Reveals

Book 3: Whiskey Undone

The Talon Pack:

Book 1: Tattered Loyalties

Book 2: An Alpha's Choice

Book 3: Mated in Mist

Book 4: Wolf Betrayed

Book 5: Fractured Silence

Book 6: Destiny Disgraced

Book 7: Eternal Mourning

Book 8: Strength Enduring

Book 9: Forever Broken

Redwood Pack Series:

Book 1: An Alpha's Path

Book 2: A Taste for a Mate

Book 3: Trinity Bound

Redwood Pack Box Set (Contains Books 1-3)

Book 3.5: A Night Away

Book 4: Enforcer's Redemption

Book 4.5: Blurred Expectations

Book 4.7: Forgiveness

Book 5: Shattered Emotions

Book 6: Hidden Destiny

Book 6.5: A Beta's Haven

Book 7: Fighting Fate

Book 7.5: Loving the Omega

Book 7.7: The Hunted Heart

Book 8: Wicked Wolf

The Complete Redwood Pack Box Set (Contains Books 1-7.7)

The Branded Pack Series:
(Written with Alexandra Ivy)
Book 1: <u>Stolen and Forgiven</u>

Book 2: Abandoned and Unseen

Book 3: Buried and Shadowed

Dante's Circle Series:
Book 1: Dust of My Wings

Book 2: Her Warriors' Three Wishes

Book 3: An Unlucky Moon

The Dante's Circle Box Set (Contains Books 1-3)

Book 3.5: His Choice

Book 4: Tangled Innocence

Book 5: Fierce Enchantment

Book 6: An Immortal's Song

Book 7: Prowled Darkness

The Complete Dante's Circle Series (Contains Books 1-7)

Holiday, Montana Series:

Book 1: Charmed Spirits

Book 2: Santa's Executive

Book 3: Finding Abigail

The Holiday, Montana Box Set (Contains Books 1-3)

Book 4: Her Lucky Love

Book 5: Dreams of Ivory

The Complete Holiday, Montana Box Set (Contains Books 1-5)

The Happy Ever After Series:

Flame and Ink

Ink Ever After

Single Title:

Finally Found You

EXCERPT: WHISKEY SECRETS

Next From New York Times Bestselling Author Carrie Ann Ryan's Whiskey and Lies

Whiskey Secrets

Shocking pain slammed into his skull and down his back. Dare Collins did his best not to scream in the middle of his own bar. He slowly stood up and rubbed the back of his head since he'd been distracted and hit it on the countertop. Since the thing was made of solid wood and thick as hell, he was surprised he hadn't given himself a concussion. But since he didn't see double, he had a feeling once his long night was over, he'd just have to make the throbbing go away with a glass of Macallan.

There was nothing better than a glass of smooth whiskey or an ice-cold mug of beer after a particularly long day. Which one Dare chose each night depended on not only his mood but also those around him. So was the life of a former cop turned bartender.

He had a feeling he'd be going for the whiskey and not a woman tonight—like most nights if he were honest. It had been a long day of inventory and no-show staff members. Meaning he had a headache from hell, and it looked as if he'd be working open to close when he truly didn't want to. But that's what happened when one was the owner of a bar and restaurant rather than just a manager or bartender—like he was with the Old Whiskey Restaurant and Bar.

It didn't help that his family had been in and out of the place all day for one reason or another—his brothers and parents either wanting something to eat or having a question that needed to be answered right away where a phone call or text wouldn't suffice. His mom and dad had mentioned more than once that he needed to be ready for their morning meeting, and he had a bad feeling in his gut about what that would mean for him later. But he pushed that from his thoughts because he was used to things in his life changing on a dime. He'd left the force for a reason, after all.

Enough of that.

He loved his family, he really did, but sometimes, they—his parents in particular—gave him a headache.

Since his mom and dad still ran the Old Whiskey Inn above his bar, they were constantly around, working their tails off at odd jobs that were far too hard for them at their ages, but they were all just trying to earn a living. When they weren't handling business for the inn, they were fixing problems upstairs that Dare wished they'd let him help with.

While he'd have preferred to call it a night and head back to his place a few blocks away, he knew that wouldn't happen tonight. Since his bartender, Rick, had called in sick at the last minute—as well as two of Dare's waitresses from the bar—Dare was pretty much screwed.

And if he wallowed just a little bit more, he might hear a tiny violin playing in his ear. He needed to get a grip and get over it. Working late and dealing with other people's mistakes was part of his job description, and he was usually fine with that.

Apparently, he was just a little off tonight. And since he knew himself well, he had a feeling it was because he was nearing the end of his time without his kid. Whenever he spent too many days away from Nathan, he acted like a crabby asshole. Thankfully, his weekend was coming up.

"Solving a hard math problem over there, or just daydreaming? Because that expression on your face looks like you're working your brain too hard. I'm surprised I don't see smoke coming out of your ears." Fox asked as he walked up to the bar, bringing Dare out of his thoughts. Dare had been pulling drafts and cleaning glasses mindlessly while in his head, but he was glad for the distraction, even if it annoyed him that he needed one.

Dare shook his head and flipped off his brother. "Suck me."

The bar was busy that night, so Fox sat down on one of the empty stools and grinned. "Nice way to greet your customers." He glanced over his shoulder before looking back at Dare and frowning. "Where are Rick and the rest of your staff?"

Dare barely held back a growl. "Out sick. Either there's really a twenty-four-hour stomach bug going around and I'm going to be screwed for the next couple of days, or they're all out on benders."

Fox cursed under his breath before hopping off his stool and going around the side of the large oak and maple bar to help out. That was Dare's family in a nutshell—they dropped everything whenever one of them needed help, and nobody even had to ask for it. Since Dare sucked at asking for help on a good day, he was glad that Fox knew what he needed without him having to say it.

Without asking, Fox pulled up a few drink orders and began mixing them with the skill of a long-time barkeep. Since Fox owned the small town newspaper—the Whiskey Chronicle—Dare was still surprised sometimes at how deft his younger brother was at working alongside him. Of course, even his parents, his older brother Loch, and his younger sister Tabby knew their way around the bar.

Just not as well as Dare did. Considering that this was *his* job, he was grateful for that.

He loved his family, his bar, and hell, he even loved his

little town on the outskirts of Philly. Whiskey, Pennsylvania was like most other small towns in his state where some parts were new additions, and others were old stone buildings from the Revolutionary or Civil war eras with add-ons —like his.

And with a place called Whiskey, everyone attached the label where they could. Hence the town paper, his bar, and most of the other businesses around town. Only Loch's business really stood out with Loch's Security and Gym down the street, but that was just like Loch to be a little different yet still part of the town.

Whiskey had been named as such because of its old bootlegging days. It used to be called something else, but since Prohibition, the town had changed its name and cashed in on it. Whiskey was one of the last places in the country to keep Prohibition on the books, even with the nationwide decree. They'd fought to keep booze illegal, not for puritan reasons, but because their bootlegging market had helped the township thrive. Dare knew there was a lot more to it than that, but those were the stories the leaders told the tourists, and it helped with the flare.

Whiskey was located right on the Delaware River, so it overlooked New Jersey but was still on the Pennsylvania side of things. The main bridge that connected the two states through Whiskey and Ridge on the New Jersey side was one of the tourist spots for people to drive over and walk so they could be in two states at once while over the Delaware River.

Their town was steeped in history, and close enough to where George Washington had crossed the Delaware that they were able to gain revenue on the reenactments for the tourists, thus helping keep their town afloat.

The one main road through Whiskey that not only housed Loch's and Dare's businesses but also many of the other shops and restaurants in the area, was always jammed with cars and people looking for places to parallel park. Dare's personal parking lot for the bar and inn was a hot commodity.

And while he might like time to himself some days, he knew he wouldn't trade Whiskey's feel for any other place. They were a weird little town that was a mesh of history and newcomers, and he wouldn't trade it for the world. His sister Tabby might have moved out west and found her love and her place with the Montgomerys in Denver, but Dare knew he'd only ever find his home here.

Sure, he'd had a few flings in Denver when he visited his sister, but he knew they'd never be more than one night or two. Hell, he was the king of flings these days, and that was for good reason. He didn't need commitment or attachments beyond his family and his son, Nathan.

Time with Nathan's mom had proven that to him, after all.

"You're still daydreaming over there," Fox called out from the other side of the bar. "You okay?"

Dare nodded, frowning. "Yeah, I think I need more caffeine or something since my mind keeps wandering." He pasted on his trademark grin and went to help one of the new arrivals who'd taken a seat at the bar. Dare wasn't the broody one of the family—that honor went to Loch—and he hated when he acted like it.

"What can I get you?" he asked a young couple that had taken two empty seats at the bar. They had matching wedding bands on their fingers but looked to be in their early twenties.

He couldn't imagine being married that young. Hell, he'd never been married, and he was in his mid-thirties now. He hadn't married Monica even though she'd given him Nathan, and even now, he wasn't sure they'd have ever taken that step even if they had stayed together. She had Auggie now, and he had...well, he had his bar.

That wasn't depressing at all.

"Two Yuenglings please, draft if you have it," the guy said, smiling.

Dare nodded. "Gonna need to see your IDs, but I do have it on tap for you." As Yuengling was a Pennsylvania beer, not having it outside the bottle would be stupid even in a town that prided itself on whiskey.

The couple pulled out their IDs, and Dare checked them quickly. Since both were now the ripe age of twenty-two, he went to pull them their beers and set out their check since they weren't looking to run a tab.

Another woman with long, caramel brown hair with hints of red came to sit at the edge of the bar. Her hair lay in loose waves down her back and she had on a sexy-as-fuck green dress that draped over her body to showcase sexy curves and legs that seemed to go on forever. The garment didn't have sleeves so he could see the toned muscles in her arms work as she picked up a menu to look at it. When she looked up, she gave him a dismissive glance before focusing on the menu again. He held back a sigh. Not in the mood to deal with whatever that was about, he let Fox take care of her and put her from his mind. No use dealing with a woman who clearly didn't want him near, even if it were just to take a drink order. Funny, he usually had to speak to a female before making her want him out of the picture. At least, that's what he'd learned from Monica.

And why the hell was he thinking about his ex again? He usually only thought of her in passing when he was talking to Nathan or hanging out with his kid for the one weekend a month the custody agreement let Dare have him. Having been in a dangerous job and then becoming a bartender didn't look good to some lawyers it seemed, at least when Monica had fought for full custody after Nathan was born.

He pushed those thoughts from his mind, however, not in the mood to scare anyone with a scowl on his face by remembering how his ex had looked down on him for his occupation even though she'd been happy to slum it with him when it came to getting her rocks off.

Dare went through the motions of mixing a few more drinks before leaving Fox to tend to the bar so he could go check on the restaurant part of the building.

Since the place had originally been an old stone inn on both floors instead of just the top one, it was set up a little differently than most newer buildings around town. The bar was off to one side; the restaurant area where they served delicious, higher-end entrees and tapas was on the other. Most people needed a reservation to sit down and eat in the main restaurant area, but the bar also had seating for dinner, only their menu wasn't quite as extensive and ran closer to bar food.

In the past, he'd never imagined he would be running something like this, even though his parents had run a smaller version of it when he was a kid. But none of his siblings had been interested in taking over once his parents wanted to retire from the bar part and only run the inn. When Dare decided to leave the force only a few years in, he'd found his place here, however reluctantly.

Being a cop hadn't been for him, just like being in a relationship. He'd thought he would be able to do the former, but life had taken a turn, and he'd faced his mortality far sooner than he bargained for. Apparently, being a gruff, perpetually single bar owner was more his speed, and he was pretty damn good at it, too. Most days, anyway.

His house manager over on the restaurant side was running from one thing to another, but from the outside, no one would have noticed. Claire was just that good. She was in her early fifties and already a grandmother, but she didn't look a day over thirty-five with her smooth, dark skin and bright smile. Good genes and makeup did wonders—

according to her anyway. He'd be damned if he'd say that. His mother and Tabby had taught him *something* over the years.

The restaurant was short-staffed but managing, and he was grateful he had Claire working long hours like he did. He oversaw it all, but he knew he couldn't have done it without her. After making sure she didn't need anything, he headed back to the bar to relieve Fox. The rush was finally dying down now, and his brother could just sit back and enjoy a beer since Dare knew he'd already worked a long day at the paper.

By the time the restaurant closed and the bar only held a few dwindling costumers, Dare was ready to go to bed and forget the whole lagging day. Of course, he still had to close out the two businesses and talk to both Fox and Loch since his older brother had shown up a few moments ago. Maybe he'd get them to help him close out so he wouldn't be here until midnight. He must be tired if the thought of closing out was too much for him.

"So, Rick didn't show, huh?" Loch asked as he stood up from his stool. His older brother started cleaning up beside Fox, and Dare held back a smile. He'd have to repay them in something other than beer, but he knew they were working alongside him because they were family and had the time; they weren't doing it for rewards.

"Nope. Shelly and Kayla didn't show up either." Dare resisted the urge to grind his teeth at that. "Thanks for helping. I'm exhausted and wasn't in the mood to deal with this all alone."

"That's what we're here for," Loch said with a shrug.

"By the way, you have any idea what this seven a.m. meeting tomorrow is about?" Fox asked after a moment. "They're putting Tabby on speaker phone for it and everything."

Dare let out a sigh. "I'm not in the mood to deal with any meeting that early. I have no idea what it's going to be about, but I have a bad feeling."

"Seems like they have an announcement." Loch sat back down on his stool and scrolled through his phone. He was constantly working or checking on his daughter, so his phone was strapped to him at all times. Misty had to be with Loch's best friend, Ainsley, since his brother worked that night. Ainsley helped out when Loch needed a night to work or see Dare. Loch had full custody of Misty, and being a single father wasn't easy.

Dare had a feeling no matter what his parents had to say, things were going to be rocky after the morning meeting. His parents were caring, helpful, and always wanted the best for their family. That also meant they tended to be slightly overbearing in the most loving way possible.

"Well, shit."

It looked like he'd go without whiskey *or* a woman tonight.

Of course, an image of the woman with gorgeous hair and that look of disdain filled his mind, and he held back a sigh. Once again, Dare was a glutton for punishment, even in his thoughts.

The next morning, he cupped his mug of coffee in his hands and prayed his eyes would stay open. He'd stupidly gotten caught up on paperwork the night before and was now running on about three hours of sleep.

Loch sat in one of the booths with Misty, watching as she colored in her coloring book. She was the same age as Nathan, which Dare always appreciated since the cousins could grow up like siblings—on weekends when Dare had Nathan that was. The two kids got along great, and he hoped that continued throughout the cootie phases kids seemed to get sporadically.

Fox sat next to Dare at one of the tables with his laptop open. Since his brother owned the town paper, he was always up-to-date on current events and was even now typing up something.

They had Dare's phone between them with Tabby on the other line, though she wasn't saying anything. Her fiancé, Alex, was probably near as well since those two seemed to be attached at the hip. Considering his future brother-in-law adored Tabby, Dare didn't mind that as much as he probably should have as a big brother.

The elder Collinses stood at the bar, smiles on their faces, yet Dare saw nervousness in their stances. He'd been a cop too long to miss it. They were up to something, and he had a feeling he wasn't going to like it.

"Just get it over with," Dare said, keeping his language decent—not only for Misty but also because his mother would still take him by the ear if he cursed in front of her.

But because his tone had bordered on rude, his mother still raised a brow, and he sighed. Yep, he had a really bad feeling about this.

"Good morning to you, too, Dare," Bob Collins said with a snort and shook his head. "Well, since you're all here, even our baby girl, Tabby—"

"Not a baby, Dad!" Tabby called out from the phone, and the rest of them laughed, breaking the tension slightly.

"Yeah, we're not babies," Misty put in, causing everyone to laugh even harder.

"Anyway," Barbara Collins said with a twinkle in her eye. "We have an announcement to make." She rolled her shoulders back, and Dare narrowed his eyes. "As you know, your father and I have been nearing the age of retirement for a while now, but we still wanted to run our inn as innkeepers rather that merely owners."

"Finally taking a vacation?" Dare asked. His parents worked far too hard and wouldn't let their kids help them. He'd done what he could by buying the bar from them when he retired from the force and then built the restaurant himself.

"If you'd let me finish, young man, I'd let you know," his mother said coolly, though there was still warmth in her eyes. That was his mother in a nutshell. She'd reprimand, but soothe the sting, too.

"Sorry," he mumbled, and Fox coughed to cover up a laugh. If Dare looked behind him, he figured he'd see Loch hiding a smile of his own.

Tabby laughed outright.

Damn little sisters.

"So, as I was saying, we've worked hard. But, lately, it seems like we've worked *too* hard." She looked over at his dad and smiled softly, taking her husband's hand. "It's time to make some changes around here."

Dare sat up straighter.

"We're retiring. Somewhat. The inn hasn't been doing as well as it did back when it was with your grandparents, and part of that is on the economy. But part of that is on us. What we want to do is renovate more and update the existing rooms and service. In order to do that and step back as innkeepers, we've hired a new person."

"You're kidding me, right?" Dare asked, frowning. "You can't just hire someone to take over and work in our building without even talking to us. And it's not like I have time to help her run it when she doesn't know how you like things."

"You won't be running it," Bob said calmly. "Not yet, anyway. Your mom and I haven't fully retired, and you know it. We've been running the inn for years, but now we want to step away. Something *you've* told us we should do. So, we hired someone. One who knows how to handle this kind of transition and will work with the construction crew and us.

She has a lot of experience from working in Philly and New York and will be an asset."

Dare fisted his hands by his sides and blew out a breath. They had to be fucking kidding. "It sounds like you've done your research and already made your decision. Without asking us. Without asking *me*."

His mother gave him a sad look. "We've always wanted to do this, Dare, you know that."

"Yes. But you should have talked to us. And renovating like this? I didn't know you wanted to. We could have helped." He didn't know why he was so angry, but being kept out of the loop was probably most of it.

His father signed. "We've been looking into this for years, even before you came back to Whiskey and bought the bar from us. And while it may seem like this is out of the blue, we've been doing the research for a while. Yes, we should have told you, but everything came up all at once recently, and we wanted to show you the plans when we had details rather than get your hopes up and end up not doing it."

Dare just blinked. There was so much in that statement —in *all* of those statements—that he couldn't quite process it. And though he could have yelled about any of it just then, his mind fixed on the one thing that annoyed him the most.

"So, you're going to have some city girl come into *my* place and order me around? I don't think so."

"And why not? Have a problem with listening to women?"

Dare stiffened because that last part hadn't come from his family. No. He turned toward the voice. It had come from the woman he'd seen the night before in the green dress.

And because fate liked to fuck with him, he had a feeling he knew *exactly* who this person was.

Their newly hired innkeeper.

And new thorn in his side.

Find out more in Whiskey Secrets.
To make sure you're up to date on all of Carrie Ann's releases, sign up for her mailing list HERE.

FALLEN INK

From New York Times Bestselling Author Carrie Ann Ryan's Montgomery Ink: Colorado Springs Series

FALLEN INK

The Montgomery Ink series continues with a spin-off in Colorado Springs, where a familiar Montgomery finds her place in a new tattoo shop, and in the arms of her best friend.

Adrienne Montgomery is finally living her dreams. She's opened a tattoo shop with her brother, Shep, and two of her cousins from Denver and she's ready to take the city by storm with her art—as long as she can handle the pressure. When her new neighbors decide her shop isn't a great fit for the community, however, she'll have to lean on the one person she didn't expect to fall for along the way...her best friend.

Mace Knight takes pride in two things: his art and his daughter. He knows he's taking a risk by starting over in a new shop with the Montgomerys, but the stakes are even higher when he finds himself wanting Adrienne more than he thought possible.

The two fall fast and hard but they know the rules; they can't risk their friendship, no matter how hot it is between the sheets and how many people try to stand in their way.

Find out more in FALLEN INK
To make sure you're up to date of all of Carrie Ann's releases, sign up for her mailing list HERE.

DELICATE INK

From New York Times Bestselling Author Carrie Ann Ryan's Montgomery Ink series

Delicate Ink

On the wrong side of thirty, Austin Montgomery is ready to settle down. Unfortunately, his inked sleeves and scruffy beard isn't the suave business appearance some women crave. Only finding a woman who can deal with his job, as a tattoo artist and owner of Montgomery Ink, his seven meddling siblings, and his own gruff attitude won't be easy.

Finding a man is the last thing on Sierra Elder's mind. A recent transplant to Denver, her focus is on opening her own boutique. Wanting to cover up scars that run deeper than her flesh, she finds in Austin a man that truly gets to her—in more ways than one.

Although wary, they embark on a slow, tempestuous burn of a relationship. When blasts from both their pasts intrude on their present, however, it will take more than a promise of what could be to keep them together.

Find out more in <u>DELICATE INK</u>

To make sure you're up to date on all of Carrie Ann's releases, sign up for her mailing list <u>HERE</u>.

BREAKING WITHOUT YOU

**From New York Times Bestselling Author Carrie Ann
Ryan's Fractured Connections Series**

BREAKING WITHOUT YOU

From NYT bestselling author Carrie Ann Ryan, comes a
brand new series where second chances don't come often,
and overcoming an unexpected loss means breaking everything you knew.

I fell for Cameron Connolly at the wrong time. And
when he left, I thought my life was over. But then, after the
worst happened, I truly understood what that phrase
meant. Now, he's not ready for a second chance, and I'm not
offering one. Though given that our families have been
forced together after losing one of our own, I know there's

no turning back. Not this time. Not again. Not when it comes to Cameron.

I never wanted to hurt Violet Knight, but there were reasons I had to leave all those years ago—not that she'd believe me if I told her what they were. I not only left her, I also left my foster brothers. Honestly, I didn't want to come back to Denver to help run my father's failing brewery. But when it comes to my brothers, I know I'll find a way to make it work. Perhaps I'll even earn Violet's forgiveness and face the connection we both thought long forgotten in the process. Because I wanted her then, but now I know I need her. I just hope she needs me.

Find out more in BREAKING WITHOUT YOU
To make sure you're up to date on all of Carrie Ann's releases, sign up for her mailing list HERE.

Made in the USA
Middletown, DE
07 November 2024

64105002R00168